# The Menace from Farside

# BOOKS BY IAN MCDONALD

LUNA TRILOGY
*Luna: New Moon*
*Luna: Wolf Moon*
*Luna: Moon Rising* (forthcoming)

EVERNESS SERIES
*Planesrunner*
*Be My Enemy*
*Empress of the Sun*

INDIA IN 2047
*River of Gods*
*Cyberabad Days*

CHAGA SAGA
*Chaga*
*Kirinya*
*Tendeléo's Story*

DESOLATION ROAD SERIES
*Desolation Road*

# THE MENACE
# FROM FARSIDE

IAN McDONALD

A TOM DOHERTY ASSOCIATES BOOK

NEW YORK

This is a work of fiction. All of the characters, organizations, and events portrayed in this novella are either products of the author's imagination or are used fictitiously.

THE MENACE FROM FARSIDE

Copyright © 2019 by Ian McDonald

Cover art by Richard Anderson
Cover design by Christine Foltzer

Edited by Jonathan Strahan

A Tor.com Book
Published by Tom Doherty Associates
120 Broadway
New York, NY 10271

www.tor.com

Tor® is a registered trademark of
Macmillan Publishing Group, LLC.

ISBN 978-1-250-24778-0 (ebook)
ISBN 978-1-250-24779-7 (trade paperback)

First Edition: November 2019

# The Menace from Farside

We're down in Hypatia with thirty minutes of air and the mother of radiation storms coming straight for us.

No. Let's try that again. Maybe put the air last? Down in Hypatia—maybe add a little extra detail to make that say more, like: a kilometre under the surface? Dead in the sights of the mother of radiation storms and thirty minutes of air left. *Only* thirty minutes of air left.

That's better. Makes it more, you know, dun dunh *dah*. Kaya, our Drama Colloq Enabler, says you should open with a big bang. Boom. Grab the attention, make them say, Wow, *what happens next?*

What do you mean, just start at the start and let it unfold naturally? What about tension, and plot beats, reveals, and all that? Drama and climaxes. You're a psychiatric bot, what do you know about stories? What do you mean, it's not important what happens, it's how what happens makes you feel? Where's the drama? Where's the excitement?

Okay, I'll start at the start, but my story, my way.

It's loathe at first sight.

It's New Year, in Queen of the South. On the plaza between the Taiyang Tower and Osman Tower. The plaza is full of Queeners, all looking up. The dragon race has just begun.

Understand: I approve of New Year, though what is it? Really? People being noisy and dumb and insisting on unwanted physical contact all because one date turns over to another. Personally, I prefer Zhonqiu, but let no one say that Cariad Corcoran doesn't allow people the right to celebrate. Even dragon racing. Which isn't dragons. There are no dragons. Well, there are. But they don't fly. And they're not made of paper and nano-film. But they can breathe fire, when they want to.

There are dragons racing in the sky and people dancing in the streets and I am about to meet my new stepfather.

Understand: marriages are difficult. Ring marriages are verging on stupid impossible. That's why people try them. When you grow up in one you never realise what a weird thing a ring is. Family is what you know. Family is what works.

I've lived my whole life with three parents: Laine, my birth-mother, and her two spouses—Dolores to her left, her iz, and Andros to her right, her derecho. And Andros has his two partners—Laine on his iz, Eadward on his derecho—and so it goes, link by link, marriage by marriage, all the way around the ring.

In an ideal world. And since when has the moon ever been an ideal world?

I never liked Dolores, but I did like Andros, so of course his was the link that split. I could see it hadn't been working between him and Laine for about a year, and when even Kobe notices it, then it's really, really not working. So it ended, the link split and Laine lost Andros and I lost him too without any say-so or negotiation or contract or anything. Anything.

It ended up a straight swap: Andros out, Gebre Sisay in. But Gebre didn't like Eadward as derecho, who wanted to stay with Andros, so in came Gebre's derecha Rachel, whose derecho Noam *did* like Eadward, and all the links went click click click and locked together. Sweet. Ring marriages: they're like living in a telenovela. Everybody's at something with everyone else. Gebre was university, come over from Farside to set up a new astronomy colloquium in Queen of the South. I didn't even know Laine was seeing him until she announced a shiny new relationship. New Year, new derecho stepfather. But when was Cariad Corcoran ever consulted? Never. Yet I'm expected to stand there, in the middle of all the noise and cooking smells and the body odour, with Kobe looking up at the dragons and telling me in his over-detailed way the difference between the Mackenzie kites and the Suns', and Jair off buying me horchata from the kiosk because I told him to and he needs direction in his life: expected to stand there in the middle of New Year waiting for Laine to bring her new amor over from the station. 'They're all out of horchata,' Jair says. He offers me a paper cup of pale slush. 'I got you frozo.'

I let my face say, *Frozo? You got me* frozo? Then I see that Jair isn't looking at me being annoyed and Kobe isn't gazing up at the long New Year dragons all tumbling and twining around the towers. So I turn and look where they're looking and see what they're seeing and it's Laine coming through the noisy, smelly crowd towing this middle-aged, stubble-shave-head man with a big smile. By the hand. But what I'm really looking at is what's on the end of his other hand.

A girl. A *daughter*.

He's towing a daughter.

I think—I *know*—all our mouths are open.

No one ran a daughter past *any* of us.

'Emer, Kobe, this is Gebre.' Why can't Laine learn this? Do not call me Emer. I hate the name. Hate it. 'Gebre, this is Jair, my iz's boy.'

Jair's little features fold up into sad-face, he makes a sore-paw gesture with his claw-glove. Laine: can you do nothing right? Jair's *neko*. Self-identified: neko's got rights much as I have. Not a boy, a neko. Got it? Right, so, I call Jair *he,* but that's an iz-derecha thing. That's *negotiated,* not assumed.

'And everyone,' Laine says, 'this is Sidibe.'

Sidibe Sisay. Tall and fit and tight in belly-top and party pants like a smear of body-paint. She's got boobs. Small, but boobs. I can see them. Jair can see them. Even Kobe can see them. Long lashes and big eyes; skin smooth and soft and flawless; hair in a big wedge on the top of her head. Hair I can never have in a billion years, skin that isn't pale and pasty and has *freckles*. And *boobs*.

'Close your mouth, Jair,' I order. Boys, really.

Sidibe Sisay offers a hand to me.

'Ola, Emer,' she says. 'Happy New Year.'

'So,' Laine says, pulling me and Kobe in with a Family Hug, 'Gebre and Sidibe are moving in with us.'

And the dragon race ends and the clock turns over from one tick to the next and the streamer cannons on the towers fire paperchains and lametta and balloons into the air and people are shouting and jumping up and down and kissing each other and Laine and Gebre are kissing each other and I can't look because it's disgusting and stupid; not just them, everyone in the plaza, why are you celebrating New Year, don't you know there can't be a new year because the world has just ended?

———————

So: what do you think of that for a start?

Look, I am telling it my own way. My own way is narrative. Story.

That's the way I do it, take it or leave it.

What did I feel? Isn't it obvious what I felt?

I am telling you what I felt, just in my own way. You might have to read in, right? And you need to know I never wanted to be here. And your chair smells weird anyway. This whole room smells weird, like fresh printed. And you smell weird as well. Freshly printed too.

———————

So, I'm two days into the new year 2089 and everyone knows about *that* girl from Farside. Not just Osman Tower, not just Queen: everyone. Faustini to Shackleton, Amundsen to the Palace of Eternal Light. Everyone. I can't go on the network. Everyone is talking. I can't go to the hotshop. Everyone is laughing. I can't go to colloq:

everyone is asking, *Who is she, where does she come from, who does her hair, is she moving in?*

I have an answer to that last one.

Yes.

Gebre Sisay contracts constructors to knock through from our apartment into one next door. One big happy family!

The sick feeling in my gut isn't the violation of our lovely home (though it is: this new extension? I call it the Carbuncle). It's that it smells of permanence. It smells of happy marriage contracts and Sidibe Sisay, my new step-sister: derecha forever.

---

Understand this: there are rules. I don't know what kind of wrong stuff they do at the university but this is Queen of the South, Queen of the Moon, and we have rules about what is acceptable and they do not include dancing around someone else's apartment (which it is, Carbuncle or no Carbuncle) in a sports top and offensively short shorts. There are boys here, understand?

So: we are five days into the Sisay invasion and Kobe hasn't shut his mouth once. I tell him it's embarrassing. Not to him; he doesn't understand embarrassment. Embarrassing to me. Which I have taught him to understand. No effect. The mouth stays open, catching dust. In the end I tell it makes him look stupid. Not to him, or me: to her. Still he hovers around the shared space between Castle Corcoran and the Carbuncle, waiting for Sidibe to pass through, smiling at her, standing way too close to her, asking her far too many questions. I give him extra errands to run for me. Trips to the printer, browsing for fashions I might like, preparing my material for colloquium. Kobe needs to be kept busy.

And the rules most definitely include *mind your own business*. Because you have no right, Sidibe Sisay, no right at all, to storm into my apartment and tell me to my face, 'You bully that kid.'

'Excuse me,' I say. Like that, offended. 'Excuse me? Kid?'

'Kobe. You make him run around for you and you never thank him or anything.'

And I say, 'Understand this.' And I explain very slowly that I'm doing this all for her, that Kobe latches on and doesn't go away, that he has boundary issues and that's how Kobe is so she should really be thanking me, not screaming at me.

'You should show him respect,' Sidibe says and swanks away back to the Carbuncle and this time it's my mouth open and not a word in it.

And then Jair. Oh, Jair. You are shameful. Shameful.

After his first hello on New Year's Night, he collapsed in like some kind of superdense matter and mooched around the apartment trying to drift into the edge of Sidibe's field of vision. He plays the kawaii card. He sits in corners with his knees pulled up to his chest. He crouches on ledges, paw-gloves between his feet. He curls up on loungers. He looks out windows all moody and sensitive. Always, always his hair falling over his right eye. I like him as neko—he's been it for almost a year and he's committed, though Dolores refuses to let him have surgery for the ears—but this is kitty-too-far.

This is hell. I am in hell. The thing about hell, as far as I understand from my research, is that you've done something to deserve it.

So this is worse than hell.

---

Cariad. If we're going to do this, that's what you call me. This is a negotiation, right? Everything is a negotiation. Even therapy.

Cariad. I picked the name about three lunes ago. It's taken longer than it should for everyone to use it. I need to put word around. Enforce a little.

Cariad. It means something beautiful in something Celtic.

Cariad. Say it.

Cariad. No. Not Cari*ad*. *C*ariad.

Good.

I mean: what kind of name is Emer? *Eee*-muh. Sounds like a painful spot on your guiche. With a red tip that turns white. Then bursts. You've got an Emer? Oh, vile. How did you get that?

Yes, I know Emer is Celtic. Irish. Laine tells me Irish is amazing. Freckles are Irish and they are not amazing. Emer is not amazing, Irish is not amazing. How can I be Irish? I was born in Ibn Bajja Med Centre in Queen of the South, in the Aitken Basin at the South Pole of the moon. Just because one of your ceegees comes from Ireland (you can't even see it from Queen, wrong hemisphere), how do you inherit it? What's the genes for that? My bio-father was a Real Madrid fan. That's a terrestrial soccer team. By that logic, because I share genes with him I should be a Real Madrid fan. I tried to watch Real Madrid on the network once but it was so slow and low. Ultimate Fighting: that's a sport.

I never met my father.

You're going to try and get something out of that, aren't you?

---

The delivery arrives by BALTRAN, from Farside.

'Can't you just print it?' I say.

'You don't have the tech here,' Sidibe says and sweeps into the elevator. Gob-daw and Smitten-Kitten are two steps behind her. I tell you, Cariad Corcoran is not going to be left behind, so I dash in just as the gate closes. I know about the BALTRAN: it's an essential part of our transport infrastructure, but I've never seen a station. Kobe tells me more about ballistic transport than I ever want to know as we ride the moto out to Nobile. Magnetic launchers and catchers that lob cargo containers from one to another on ballistic trajectories. BALlistic TRANsport. BALTRAN. Infrastructure is Kobe's thing. Trains, motos, tethers, rovers, rockets: he lights up.

Turns out the BALTRAN is interesting, not for the infrastructure but for the people. People can ride the cans. If they're in a hurry. You should see them when they come out: clinging to the lock walls, grey, heaving. Some have vom on their faces. Being fired around the moon on a ballistic trajectory is not stylish. It is very, very funny.

Sidibe's delivery does not have any human body fluids on it. But it is bulky. She pays the waybill and slings her delivery onto her back. It's almost as big as she is, but she moves proud, showing off, like it's some fantastic secret.

Back in the Carbunculum she unrolls it on the floor of Gebre's family space. A suit, like a sasuit but tighter and goldier. Complex folded things where a suitpack would be, but this is not a sasuit. Sidibe takes it to her room and returns in skintight glitter and gold.

Jair's eyes go wide. Another one of Dolores's directives from afar: an absolute ban on anime eyes. See you, Dolores, wherever you are: Jair has them now, over shiny Sidibe.

'Kobe, mouth,' I say.

Sidibe hooks her hands into bindings and stretches out her arms. 'I haven't room in here to unfold them fully,' she says. Wings. She's got wings. Great shimmering wings that flutter, that fill El Carbunculo's family space and shiver and tremble in the flow from the air con. She flexes her wings, sending a waft of fresh nano-filament aroma into my face.

For this is the worst, the very worst thing about Sidibe Sisay.

'You can fly,' Jair says.

'I can fly,' she agrees.

'You can't, I mean, you're from Farside, it's all tunnels and tubes,' I say. 'I mean, where is there to fly?' Then I bite the inside of my mouth because I have just handed Sidibe victory over my boys.

'I'll arrange a demonstration,' she says and folds her wings and slips back to her room to change out of the flight suit.

'Your ass looks big in that,' I shout after her.

---

So we all have to watch Sidibe Sisay fly.

Gebre takes us all in the construction elevator up the side of Osman Tower, right to the very top. We all wear safety harnesses and are told to clip on before we clip off. I'm good with that. I don't find that patronising, not at all. Safety at heights is a good thing.

Such things do not apply to Sidibe. She prances around in her clingy gold suit, pretending to be excited and nervous. Looking down, I feel sick, even clipped to a construction beam. It's two kilometres to the floor of Queen of the South. Looking up is worse: I see the sun panels, the girders reaching for the roof, and feel like I'm falling backwards. So I keep my eye on Kobe because he just might unclip his harness for some reason in his little logic. Jair is comfortable and easy at height. Relaxed, flexed. Cute.

Gebre hugs Sidibe, then she steps to the edge and flexes her arms. Her wings snap out from the pack and lock. Up here she can open them fully and she's almost as wide as the whole tower. Everyone but me goes ooh. Then she throws her head back, lifts her arm-wings, and falls forward into space.

I gasp with everyone else. I admit it. Anyone would. Everyone but me lunges forward to see what has happened. I grab Kobe's tether, just to be sure. Jair grips a girder and leans out over the drop. I can't look. I'm still coming to terms with what I just saw. She threw herself off the top of Osman Tower. Then Sidibe soars up over, over the edge of the platform, and climbs high above us. She is shining and gold. She flaps her wings. Her feathers catch the sunline and flash it into our eyes. She burns. She is an angel. She spins on a wingtip and in a breath is a kilometre away. Two wingbeats and she wheels around the soaring spike of Kingscourt across the plaza. She tucks her wings and flips into a dive. We all strain our tethers to see where she has gone. Sidibe pulls out of her dive, scrapes the tops of the trees that line the Boulevard of Heavenly Peace. All Queen of the South can see her. The entire city is watching. Another flash of light: wingbeats catching the sun. Another banked turn and now she's spiralling up around Taiyang Tower like a golden ribbon winding around an arm. She swoops across two cubic kilometres of air, then flashes up over the edge of our home tower once again, hangs a moment, folds her wings, and lands light as a breath on the tower top.

Gebre hugs her hard. She complains: *Mind the wings the wings.*

Laine says: *That was amazing, amazing.*

Jair: *That was cool, really cool. Coolest thing I ever saw.* For Jair, that's really losing his shit.

Kobe: *That was one of the greatest things I have ever seen.* Sometimes the way he says whatever is in his head is mortifying, sometimes it's beautiful. With Kobe you have to learn his patterns. Whatever he says, it's always honest.

Me? I hug her. *That was amazing,* I say. And it was. I cannot deny it. Sidibe has won. Sidibe has won big. But this is only a battle. The war is far from over, and only ultimate victory counts. I stand at the back of the elevator as we ride back down the side of Osman Tower so she can't try to read my face. Her ass still looks big in that flying suit.

———

That night Gebre insists we all go out to eat. Not a hotshop, no. A proper restaurant: recreational eating. Birthdays and death-days and exam-passing eating. Watch-my-daughter-fly eating. Food you eat with chopsticks, not fingers. Red lanterns and red ropes and red seats. Servers who don't know you and are so polite you want to trip them up. There is meat on the menu. Real dead-animal meat.

*Ikh,* Jair says, folding his hands in front of his face to show his disgust.

'I thought cats were supposed to be carnivores,' Gebre says. This is meant to be a joke, but Jair shoots him an under-fringe glare like a meteor strike. I could hug my little neko for that death-glare.

'Have whatever you want,' Gebre says, trying to recover. 'My treat.'

It is then that the sense of creeping wrong that has been crawling closer ever since the boss server or whatever they call them showed us to our plush family booth arrives and throws an arm around my throat. Gebre is smiling. Sidibe is smiling. Laine is smiling. All I can see are the smiles, and then the smiles join up teeth and lips into one horror-smile that opens into a black hole to absolute sucking nothing.

This isn't a celebration of the Amazing Flying Sidibe Sister.

This is something much, much worse.

I force the food down, mouthful by mouthful. Everything looks like jewels and tastes like dust. Each mouthful is harder than the last until I am almost gagging on the dread. I am sick inside, sick with anticipation, sick with the anxiety that it will come back up, sick waiting waiting waiting for the hammer to fall. I look at Jair and Kobe. Kobe is happy prodding meat into his mouth, enjoying the new taste and texture. He will pay for that later. But Jair smells something off. He looks over at me, cute-frowns, but I can give him nothing back, not a word, not a look, not even a twitch, because that Sidibe Sisay has me in her sights and will kill me with a chopstick through the eye if I as much as squeak what I know is going to happen.

Gebre orders the vodka. A flask, the restaurant's own distillation. So cold there is ice on the outside. Frozen glasses, too, one for each of us. Smoking under the red lanterns. Gebre pours and the vodka is thick and slow as oil.

'Kobe doesn't drink,' I say and I am amazed I even get the words out.

'Just taste it, Kobe,' Laine says and suddenly everything is clear and calm and colder than the Red Carp's frozen vodka. This is a toast.

Laine's looking at Gebre. Gebre's looking at Laine all shy and coy. Sidibe is grinning like Qingzhao in colloq's pet ferret, after it ate Sean's ferret's babies. Maybe even more predatory.

'Okay, well, we have an announcement,' Laine says. 'Raise your glasses.'

I watch my fingers lift the glass and leave two circles of meltwater in the frost.

'Gebre and I,' Laine says.

'Me and Laine,' Gebre says. 'We're going to . . .'

'Get married,' they say together.

Laine and Gebre are smiling, though the smiles are melting as fast as the ice on the Red Carp's vodka. Jair's eyes are like holes in reality. Kobe looks about to break into the Storm, the thing he does when new things happen and he can't process them. I take his hand, hold it firm and tight. The pressure reassures him. I have no idea what my face looks like, but I'm hoping it's some acceptable version of happy. From Sidibe's expression I think it's anything but. Everything hangs for a hideous moment. Then Sidibe knocks back her vodka and throws her glass across the room.

'To us!'

Laine drinks, Gebre drinks; glasses fly. Jair summons the cat within, downs the glass in one, and flings the glass. Kobe lifts his glass, I take it from him and down it myself before he can drink it. I make sure to give the empty shot back to him. He throws it with great energy and no accuracy. Then I down mine, reel a bit from the double hit, and my glass joins the shards in the corner.

'May the ring be unbroken!' I shout.

Now the entire restaurant is on its feet, everyone shouting, *May the ring . . .* and toasting and flinging whatever they can find—glasses, tea glasses, bowls—into the corner. Bots whisk out to sweep and scoop the pile of broken glass and it becomes a game of target-the-bot and the whole restaurant and its red lanterns and red ropes and red chairs is full of shouts and cheers and flying crockery and polite, polite staff losing their polite. Laine and Gebre smile and wave and drink down the applause and it makes them more dizzy and drunk than any restaurant vodka. Laine can't see me looking at her. What I see is her more happy, more filled with laughing and joy and brightness, than I have seen her in years and the universe has ended and what lies beyond is nothing but sharp, grinding darkness but I can't take that joy away from her.

---

I have twenty days to save my family.

Twenty days: then the entire Oruka Ring will contract from the width of the whole moon to a tight band around Osman Tower. They'll come by train and rover-bus and BALTRAN: from St Olga and Hypatia, from Twé and Hadley, from Nearside and Farside. They'll come and they'll print out best clothes and best scents and best hair-dos. Then we'll all go together hand-in-hand to the Yuyuan Garden and in the Pavilion of Celestial Joy Laine and Gebre will sign wedding contracts.

And Sidibe Sisay will be my derecha forever and ever.

I have no words. None.

The nearer links have already been over. Dolores has called in from wherever the fuck it is she goes when Jair gets too much trouble for her. Two visits. A record for Dolores. First visit to see who these new people in her derecha's apartment are, second visit to find out if there's any dirt she can get on them. Jair makes sure he's visiting his iz Esteban if Dolores is even in the same quartersphere.

I need to do something. What can I do?

I'm not stupid enough to try and split Laine and Gebre up.

Bullet point one: it won't work.

Bullet point two: it will get me fired right across the ring to the furthest possible person with a ceegee contract and I will be exiled there until I die of lousy frozen virginity.

Twenty days to take back control of my crazy family.

Wait. Take back control.

———

Dolores. I don't like her. And?

No one ever said ring marriages were perfect. What marriage is? What family is? You get all these telenovelas—Laine loves them, I watch them so I have something to sneer about in colloq—and they always say, dysfunctional St Olga family the Komarovs; dysfunctional Hadley family the Thomases . . . And I watch, because these telenovela folk: they're clever, they construct them to draw you in even if you hate the characters. So I watch these dysfunctional families and I see people who love and can't bear each other, who have to be close and can't live with each other, who would do anything for these people they love and who can be so weak and shameful. I watch them and I don't see anything more dysfunctional than the families of my colloq-folk. My own family. What do you expect? Perfection? This is people we're talking about.

Dolores: whatever she and Laine had, I can't remember it. It's gone, and if she were any kind of right human being, she'd be gone too, break the link, move across the ring. Or even just shoot right out of it. Laine has always liked Esteban; they could just get together and close up the ring.

She treats Laine wrong: that's why I don't like her.

And she treats Jair worse.

What do you mean, lack of woman role models in my life?

---

'There's a footprint out there in the Sea of Tranquility,' I say.

We're in the sauna at the Prince Igor banya; Jair, Kobe, Sidibe, and me. I've booked a private suite at the baths as a kind of pre-wedding present to Sidibe. That's what I want her to think. What I really want is to lull her with hot water and oils and steam and shit so she can't say no to my pitch. Sidibe has never been to a real banya and there is nothing like Prince Igor on Farside. I know because I've researched this. Research stuff. That is how you know things.

'The first footprint on the moon,' I say.

The sauna is a little wooden box, just big enough for Sidibe to sprawl out on a bench. I love the smell of hot wood. Now that the Asamoahs can grow it, it's not so rare, but it still makes me feel strange, not comfortable in my skin. The moon is rock and metal, glass and dust. This is not a moon of wood. Kobe sits by the door. He likes to know where the exits are. Jair is wrapped up in a sheet, perched on the upper bench, but he looks as pale and cool as ever, though the heat is ferocious. He has body issues, but he has managed to do something with his hair to make it look like neko-ears. I admire that. Sidibe is amazing. Even when sweating. I got a private sauna cabin because Kobe can't be trusted not to say something inappropriate in public, and Jair won't even wear a sheet when other people are watching, but mostly to keep people from paying attention to Sidibe.

I have better muscle definition, though.

'The first Apollo,' I say.

Kobe looks up and I see him take a breath to correct or explain something. I lift a finger. It has taken time, but he now understands the instruction. *Too much detail, Kobe.* He shifts on the bench, but he does not interrupt.

'One hundred years ago the first humans landed on the moon,' I say. 'In the Sea of Tranquility. The first footprint belonged to a man called Neil Armstrong.' Sidibe props herself up on her elbows. 'He came down the ladder, and put his foot on the surface and said, *"It's one small step for a man, one giant leap for humanity."* That footprint—the first footprint on the moon—is still there. On the Sea of Tranquility.'

I leap up and dash to the cold pool and jump in with a big yell. Sidibe is two steps beyond me. We slop water all around the tiny polished stone chamber.

'How can it still be there?' Sidibe asks.

'Footprints last forever,' I say. The cold is digging in now, little daggers. 'That footprint can last ten million years.'

Everyone knows about King Dong, the hundred-kilometre-high spunking cock and balls that bored Mackenzie jackaroos stomped into Oceanus Procellarum with boots and rover tracks. I'm related to one of the original makers. I'm proud of that.

'But they blasted off again,' Sidibe says. 'That's your footprint, whoof!'

A huge splash that half empties the cold pool. Water backwashes from the walls onto us; waves of colder-than-cold. We yell. Kobe bobs up, hair streaming.

'The Apollo lunar modules were built in two stages,' he says. My teeth are chattering, but Kobe, he just doesn't feel the cold. 'The descent stage was abandoned for lunar liftoff and rendezvous with the command module. Therefore the blast went out.' He demonstrates with his arms and sends a chilly rain across the cold room. 'Boof!'

'So.' My teeth are chattering. 'All the footprints are still there. Including . . .'

'The original!' Sidibe says.

Got her.

I haul myself out of the splash pool and rush blue-assed into the steam room. Jair is already there, like a duster who has dumped their clothes after a party. He didn't join us in the plunge. Nekos don't do cold.

I arrange myself on the top tier. Sidibe lies on her back on the moonstone slab, one knee cocked, one arm folded behind her head as a pillow. Kobe pours water onto hot rock. He loves to hear the hiss and see the steam fill the room. The wave of heat almost takes my breath away. Almost.

'I think,' I say very slowly, so there can be no misunderstanding, 'we should go there.'

Sidibe sits up.

'What?'

'I think we should go there. All of us.' Jair looks up. Kobe's hand stops halfway to the water scoop.

'All of us?' Jair says.

'All of us,' I say. 'Me, you, Kobe. Sidibe.'

'Why would I want to go to Kneel Strong-arm's footprint?' Sidibe asks.

I let the obvious error go, because here is the genius. The bit that kept me up until four in the morning, trying to get the key that would lock it all together.

'For a wedding present,' I say.

Oh, I am brim-full of clever. Research research research. First the Armstrong footprint, then, once I knew that the wedding card was the one to play, the whole wedding-present thing. I explain to my expedition—see, in my head we are adventuring, bound for the Sea of Tranquility—about giving gifts to people getting married. It's not a thing we do—why give someone something when they can print out anything they want, and not take up any precious carbon allocation? But on Earth, folk get so many wedding presents they're like showers.

'It'd be something special just for Laine and Gebre,' I

say. 'Something no one else can give them.'

I have to be careful here. Sidibe is frowning. I don't want to oversell this.

'Couldn't we just make a cake?' Jair asks.

I turn on him.

'Can you get wheat flour? Can you get eggs, milk, all that? Do you know anyone has a bake-oven? Can you even bake?'

He shrinks. Sorry, Jair; I had to do it.

'We make it special so it's just from us,' I say. 'We print a little marker with their names on it, or a flag, and leave it there and take a picture of all of us with it. We did this, for you.'

Sidibe knows I have a scheme but she can't see it. Now I have to nail her down.

'It would be an expedition,' I say. 'A proper adventure.'

'Adventure,' Jair says. 'Isn't that really just another name for dangerous?'

'I know where to go, and we'd plan it properly,' I say. 'But dangerous? Yes, enough to make it something really precious.' There's a new meme in colloq and in the hot-shops; a woman's head, left half black skin, right half white bone. Half living, half skeleton. You can wear her as a charm on a bracelet on an arm or an ankle, around the neck, in the ear or the brow, you can have her as a pin or a brooch, or a print on a shirt or a top or the ass of your leggings. They call her Lady Luna. Saint and goddess, demon, angel, friend and enemy. Life and death. Giver and taker. But she's more than those things. Those are human things. She isn't human: Lady Luna is the moon. I haven't rushed to get my Lady Luna tee or shorts or nose-pin because that's what everyone else is doing, but I understand her. She is the edge of danger in my plan that makes it exciting. 'When were you last on the surface? Kobe? Jair? Sidibe?' I don't give them a chance to answer because it was what's called a *rhetorical question* and anyway they can all give the same answer: *Same as you, Cariad.*

For your tenth birthday you get given a sasuit and you hide your disappointment but put it on for the picture with your helmet under your arm. There's Laine, grinning, there's me, a bit furious. Brave little jackaroo. With the suit, you get suit training. You get sent to suitschool and they show you how to squeeze into it proper and hook it all up and bring it to life. Then they take you into one of the big locks. You put your hand on the shoulder of the suit in front of you and you shuffle into the chamber. You can't tell when it deepees—the gate opens and you shuffle a bit more and you are out on the surface. Instead of a shoulder you're holding a safety line. Maybe the Earth is bright and that is a thing to see. Otherwise you shuffle around your half-kay loop under the lights, back into the lock again, and like most people never go up to the surface again. You take off your suit and you put it away in a closet and forget about the Worst Birthday Ever. You can't recycle it for carbon because you never know when you might need it for the Thing Terrible. Says Cariad Corcoran: any Thing Terrible enough to threaten Queen of the South isn't going to wait while you say, *Half a minute, I just need to go and find where I put my sasuit.* Lady Luna knows a thousand ways to kill you: that's the meme.

'We all go on about how we're the first generation to live on the moon. We don't. We live *in* the moon. We're born in holes and caves and we live in holes and caves and think that's the moon but it isn't even a tiny part of the moon. The moon is up there. That's our world, and we should walk on it and claim it and make it ours. Come out of our holes and caves and say, *This is our world.* Put our footprints next to the ones that came from Earth. Neil and me. Neil and Kobe, Neil and Jair, Neil and Sidibe.'

Every pitch has three parts. Andros taught me all about this, before the split with Laine. He worked in media: everything is a pitch. The first part is the hook. You tell the pitchee something that makes them curious. Could be a question, could be a fact that not a lot of people know, could be a single brilliant image. But it makes them want to know more. The second part is the gleam. You answer your question, you unfold your fact, you shine up your image until it's blinding. You draw your pitchee in, make them see what you see, feel what you feel. Understand, it's not about a brilliant idea or a fantastic feature or even changing the world. It's about feeling. Emotion emotion emotion: all the way up, all the way down. And I have the gleam. Oh, small gods and Mary, I have the gleam. Kobe would walk straight out of the banya and into an outlook. Jair is all huddled up in his sheet but I can see him swallowing a lump in his throat. And Sidibe ... Sidibe. She is bolt upright now, leaning forward, eyes and nostrils wide. I have her. Yes, you can fly, but you fly in a cave. This is a whole world, if you're brave enough.

And now the third part of the pitch: the deal. You offer something—a new software suite, fruit, a news story, a telenovela storyline. The chance to go somewhere no kid ever went before. In return: the agreement. I will buy, I will eat, I will read your story, watch your show. I will go on your adventure.

'So, are you coming with me?'

And they all shout, *Yes, we are!*

---

The true leader never has doubts.

The true leader considers practicalities, realities, deliverability. That was one of Andros's favourite words. Deliverability. A pitch is only as good as what you can deliver. I was never sure why he left the ring. Laine never told me. One day I had a derecho-ceegee, then I was floating around the divorce party in a Kingo dress from the 2020s. He left a hole nearly a year wide.

Laine really needs to tell me things.

So: it's fourteen days to Operation First Footprint, and we have practicalities and planning.

Kobe appoints himself Department of Transport. He produces heavily-detailed presentations of train times, passenger and commercial; and the models, features, and spec of rovers. Everything except how to get one.

Sidibe puts herself in charge of surface activity on the principle of what I call Peril Suits. Wings are perilous, so are sasuits. If she's good at one, she must be good at the other. I suspect her logic, but I'm happy to let her do it as long as she doesn't assume that Peril Suits include things like navigating or giving orders. Suits, air, water, power, food: those are hers. The adventure stuff is *mine*.

I put Jair in charge of security. He's good with things that think. He's anonymized our locations, set up some code to disguise our search history, and has us meet in a different hotshop from the ones we eat in every day.

And that's his contribution to Operation First Footprint security. Even Kobe can see that Jair isn't really in. Here is danger. If one person drops out—if one person isn't staunch—the whole adventure falls apart.

We work hard and fast. Wedding-minus-eighteen now. Two days gone deciding who does what and, more important, who doesn't do what. Triangle of Production. Three corners: Good, Fast, Cheap. You can have any two but not the third. Another one of Andros's teachings. We can do fast and cheap. I tell everyone good will follow, sure as dark Earth follows light. I'm hoping Laine or Gebre are too busy planning for the wedding to ask us exactly what we're doing. Cariad Corcoran's Corollary to the Triangle of Production. You can have it good, fast, or quiet. If you can't get quiet, then get a wedding. The best place to hide any secret is inside a wedding.

———————

I know. There's no other side, there's no near and far. It's not literally a ring. It's a network of contracted marriages and nurturing relationships, a special form of polyamory where each member is married to two spouses, an iz and a derecho, who in turn are married to an iz or a derecho, and so on, to the left, to the right, until the ring comes full circle. I live in one, right? You're a psychiatric bot. Of course you know how it works, but you don't know how it feels. You wanted to know how it makes me feel.

It feels like a ring that goes right around the world. Wherever I go, Hadley or Twé or even Farside, there will be an Oruka there. I'm in it and inside it at the same time. Can you understand that? It's one thing, a whole thing. It's like surface tension in a bubble—I learned about that. It wants to pull inwards, pull together and be whole. When Andros divorced and moved across the ring, Laine was itchy and twitchy for a long time. I'm pretty sure Reuben, his derecho, felt the same too, though I don't know him or his kids all that well.

Oh, they were talking to you?

What did they say about me?

Fuck your professional etiquette. You don't even know what that means.

It's not easy being in a ring. It's complicated. People are always complicated. It's got one great feature: it's good for kids—it evolved to provide kids with a super-stable support system. SSSS. Ssss. It may be the greatest support network for kids ever invented. The moon is hard on kids. It's harder on love. In fact, I'd say that when it comes to love, rings are the craziest of all possible families, apart from all the others.

---

And now it's two days to Operation First Footprint.

How did that happen?

I mean, those days: where did they go?

Sidibe calls a suit inspection.

We gather after hours in the common room in the colloquium house. It's never completely empty: there is a pack of table-gamers down the hall, but they are (a) noisy and (b) intent, so we could be building a second sun in our room and they would never notice.

Suit up.

Now, I rock the surface activity suit look. The tight weave works well on curvy girls with good muscle definition. I've given mine a sneaky custom job, highlighted the muscle lines with red. I'm hot, but commanding. Sidibe of course is a vision in gold, but she looks like someone cosplaying a character in one of those kid telenovelas that are all about the relationships because the budget won't run to surface shooting. She looks like Awusi Sarfo in *Glass Hearts*. I look like a jackaroo.

My eyes! Kobe waddles in wearing white and high-visibility orange. Good, fast, quiet just got run into the dust by good, fast, gaudy. He is visible from orbit. This, he tells me, is his plan: he and his little friend Chao have been working on a special adventure-proof suit. They've added emergency devices and backups and trackers and comms until he stands before us in the safest sasuit ever to step out of Shoemaker Main Lock. If anything does happen, he'll be noticed and found in less than a minute.

'Kobe Kobe Kobe,' I say. 'Understand this. The thing—the entire thing—is not to be noticed.'

This time Sidibe sides with me.

'Plus, Kobe? Your friend Chao?'

'Oh,' says Kobe.

Oh, indeed.

Sasuits: the thing. You're out there in what looks like sports gear, because the whole idea is that the tight weave allows you to move free as a dancer. You're kind of wearing your own skin. Like your own skin, it's your responsibility. There is your danger. I can't trust Kobe not to get over-interested in some surface detail and forget where he is and what is—or isn't—around him. I wanted him in an old-school armoured suit. It does everything for you.

'Kobe: think about this,' I say. 'I'd like you in a shell-suit. You can still have all your alarms and surprises; sure. But we need one person we can rely on. Can you be that person?'

See, Sidibe? I asked sweet. I didn't bully. I persuaded. While being commanding.

Jair arrives in black and drapery.

'This is a suit inspection,' Sidibe says. Jair crouches on a chair and this time the cute-neko does not work with

Sidibe or with me. 'That is not a suit. That is scarves. Where is your suit?' I have not seen Sidibe angry before. She is impressive. But she doesn't know him like I do and so she can't see that at any moment he might say fuck it and there will be no Adventure.

'Sidibe, we're good,' I say.

'We're good when I say we're good. I said a suit inspection . . .'

She's not hearing me. She needs to hear me.

'Sidibe,' I say, 'we're good.'

She flounces her hair and stomps off in shiny gold. Then Jair slips off his chair and wraps his scarves around his face until only his eyes show. Through all this Kobe has been looking more and more unhappy until he too walks out and it's just Cariad Corcoran presenting for suit inspection. Two days to Adventure and my team is in bits. These people need to understand discipline. These people need to understand the chain of command.

———

Understand this: I've researched you. I know how you neo-Freudians operate. Kill popa, fuck moma. Fuck popa, kill moma. That's your theory? Of how human heads work? I mean, it's not just that it's icky; it's that your idea of family and parents are so *ancient*. So *binary*.

Bio-parent is family-parent. That's all you need to know everything about people.

Well, machine, I'm here to open up your head. Or casing, or whatever. Pop your cloud.

In rings, you have bio-parents and you have ceegees. Caregivers. They can be the same, but they don't have to be. You can only be married to the people on either side of you, but anyone in the ring can be a ceegee. To anyone. Doesn't matter how young or old you are.

That's how come Kobe lives with us. He's not related to me gene-wise, but Laine is his ceegee. It all happened eight years go. Someone three links to the derecho was going away to work on the Meridian build and couldn't find anyone to care for her boy. Laine was the only one not running off somewhere to extract something or engineer somewhere so she took him in. Then the someone died. The link closed. Doesn't always happen that way and it's cute when it does, but the new iz and derecha couldn't agree about who would care for Kobe and anyway he was settled here and Laine liked him and I was kind of used to him and his neuro-atypicalities. So he stayed.

What I'm saying is, rings care.

What I'm really saying is, Freud was a dick.

———————

Right, so: Cariad Corcoran needs to talk her team down.

Kobe is back at the apartment in his den. He is still in his glo-suit, in a corner, the quilt off his bed wrapped around him like a cloak. I will overlook the security breach of him taking the elevator up from colloq in That Suit. The mission itself is in peril. I crouch down and play-punch him on the shoulder. That is a thing that really grounds him.

'Thanks for agreeing to the shell-suit, Kobe. I know you really love this gear, but I need you to be security and rescue. If anything happens, we'll need you, Kobe.'

He opens his quilt like Sidibe opening her wings. I slip inside, beside.

'Is Jair going to go?'

'We all go, or no one goes.'

'But if Jair doesn't want to go, then we can't go.'

'Jair will go.'

'How can you be sure?'

'I have the word for Jair.'

'No offence, Cariad, but what if he doesn't want to hear your word?'

'Deep down, Jair wants to go.'

'How do you know that?'

'Because it would make him look bad to Sidibe.'

'Why is it important that he looks good to Sidibe?'

'Let's just say he needs it.'

'Is this an iz-derecha thing?'

'I think it is, Kobe.'

Kobe leans against me. I know his language, his ways, I lean back.

'I think you can do this, Cariad.'

'Thank you, Kobe. I do need to go talk to Jair now. Are you all right here?'

'I'm all right here, Cariad.'

'That's good. I'll not be long. One thing? Put something else on. If Laine finds you in that suit, there is no First Footprint.'

———————

Chidozie in our hotshop does these great yam-cakes.

Oh yes, I forgot. You only know what that's like, not what it is.

So let me tell you, she shreds them real fine, and soaks out most—but not all—of the starch. That's the important part because it's the starch that gives them stick so they don't fall apart, and it's the starch that goes crispy around the edge, because there is nothing better than crispy.

You'll have to believe me on that.

To be honest with you, there's not that much to a yam-cake. It's the dipping sauces that make it interesting.

Those and the crispy edge.

Why am I telling you this?

Because there is this thing you do, like a little blink, or a breath, or a pause, when you hit something that tickles your theory-routine. You don't have to do it; they could have coded you without that so I can only think that it's there for a reason. The most obvious reason would be to get me to say more, but that's the obvious reason and Cariad Corcoran has always been the one who lifts the corner of the obvious to see what's underneath. You did it when I was telling you about Jair and Sidibe. Like a little click. Tic.

Understand, I'm thinking you're trying to push your theory onto my family. And it doesn't fit. Like a sasuit that's too small. The rules are clear. You can be with anyone you like in the ring, except your iz-sib and your derecho-sib.

Yes, I know Jair and Sidibe aren't directly related. Yes, I know links split and reform. Isn't that what this is about? But it's like Chidozie's yam-cakes. It's the crunchy bits around the edges that are interesting.

And yes, when I said that thing about you being coded: yes; I intended to deny you agency.

---

And so Jair.

Have I told how much he annoys me? Everything he says, he does, he is, is infuriating. He thinks he can get away with it because he's cute but, Jair? Even your cute is infuriating. Because it's cute.

He's in what I call Number Three Neko Nest. That's the one on the balcony. He had his legs through the railing. A kilometre below his claw-booties are the treetops of city floor. He knows it fazes me—that's why he's there. I can imagine sliding through the rails (How? Magic, horror, something impossible?) and falling. Did I tell you how infuriating Jair is?

I look at his ears. Eye contact spooks Jair.

'Understand this: she will go without you.'

'She wouldn't do that.'

'She really wants to go. Believe.'

'I thought the rules were we all go or no one goes.'

'All right, then. If we don't go because you're scared to, how do you think she'll feel? How do you think she'll see you?'

'I'm not scared.'

'She'll think you are.'

'It doesn't matter to me what she thinks.' He hunches his shoulders and swings his feet over the drop. My stomach gives a little twitch but I glow inside. There, right there, Cariad Corcoran wins.

'You have got a suit, haven't you, Jair?'

'Of course I've got a suit. Everyone's got a suit.'

And he'll look cute in that too, I doubt not. And I don't care, as long as he turns up in it.

———————

And now, Cariad Corcoran's finishing move. I go over to the Carbuncle shouting names and trying to be cool about the wedding checklists stuck to the wall, but Gebre is out and golden Sidibe is not in her eyrie. I find her in the Alcalde Hotshop on Divine Harmony Plaza having tea like any sane person. The Alcalde is the flyers' hotshop. She's drifted into the flying circle—most of them are older than her, which I don't like—but it's good she's making her own friends. You can tell flyers from a way off. They have this profile, this silhouette. Pecs, abs, bis, and tris: they have amazing upper body development. I have curves, but I still go right into their little conclave. You may have the arm definition but I have the *stance*. Sidibe sees me, finishes up, and we go out onto the plaza.

'That was rude, Emer.'

'Are you staunch?'

'What?

'Are you staunch?' I like that word. It's a jackaroo word; I got it from Marisa Mackenzie across the ring.

She's an engineer on that crazy train thing they're building with the Vorontsovs. It's the great Mackenzie virtue: staunch. It sounds righteous and solid, like God's guts.

'Why are you asking me?'

'Are you staunch?'

'Has someone been saying stuff about me?'

'Are you staunch?'

Third time is the charm or the betrayal.

'I'm staunch, Emer.'

I hold it a moment.

'That's all I need.'

I walk away. My walkaway is almost as good as my stance. I never doubted Sidibe was staunch. Of all of them, Sidibe is the most true. But I have to make her prove it to herself. For a moment I'm tempted to look back to see the puzzlement on the faces of her flying friends, but looking back is always a weak move.

———————

And now it's no more days to Operation First Footprint.

———————

Sidibe is solid gold but I am a boss in white and red. Sidibe suggested we stow the suits at the Alcalde. So we step out from the back room like two track queens, fingers of the left hand hooked through the webbing handles of the suitpack, helmet cradled under the right arm, proper duster style. Every flyer turns to stare at us as we cruise past. We pretend to notice them out of the corners of our eyes. What we're really looking at is each other.

Jesus and Mary, we're hot.

A moto circles in across the plaza to stop in front of us. My heart is in my throat and my belly in my moonboots. They've found us. They knew all along. They were letting us run out to the end of our tether. Now they're pulling us in. The moto unfolds its panels. Jair stands up among the open shells. He's long and skinny in pink and purple tiger stripes. The toes of his moonboots and tips of his glove fingers are little fast-print claws. His helmet has ears. Furry ears. Those are going to gather a lot of dust out there.

Don't care. I want to jump up and down. I want to kiss him. He is gorgeous and he is cute and he is here here here.

'Get in,' he says. We bounce in beside him. Sidibe's squadron are on their feet, mouths open as the moto closes up around us. We look like some kind of gods. Truth? There's not a lot of space in a Queen of the South moto with three First Footprint adventurers. I've got suitpacks and helmets on my knee, Sidibe is curled into the space behind the seats.

'How did you get this?' I ask as Jair gives the instruction and we rake off across Divine Harmony Plaza.

'Cloned Dolores's log-ins and privileges,' he says. 'I told her, I told her, I told her: biometric. Always biometric. But she's so stupid-lazy.'

'So you've access to . . . ?' I ask.

'Everything,' Jair says. As a structural engineer, Dolores's everything means whatever rolls or walks or crawls or flies upon the moon.

So we go: in and out of the traffic, across the big boulevards and plazas. We drive away from the handful of towers of city core, out to where the city shrinks and the roof of the lava bubble and the floor come together. See: if we went to Queen Station, in this gear, there would be private security waiting for us at Meridian Station to turn us right round and put us on the next train back to Laine and Gebre. Of course there would. Any responsible ceegee would do that.

But we aren't going to Queen Station. Oh no.

My Department of Transport can be a real schemer when you explain the stakes to him.

The further from the centre of Queen, the more the city becomes a construction site. Bots, graders, sinterers. Cranes swinging beams, manipulators. Everywhere the spiky blue light of welding. Humans shouldn't be here, humans are in the way. Humans could get hurt. Our little moto steers between the machines and the swinging aluminium and glass. The dust thickens until it's hard to see. The moto is a little bubble inside grey, greyer, and greymost. Shapes and things materialise, loom, and dissolve. Moondust is dark and treacherous stuff. My five-derecho died from silicosis. Thirty-five. Laine says that's no age at all. I went to the memorial. Everyone whispered that the zabbaleen wouldn't recycle her lungs. Moondust had turned them to stone. And this same dust is wisping in through the air vents.

'Helmets!' Sidibe says. Beats me to it by a hair. I clap mine around my head, the helmet clams shut, I feel the seal link with the suit ring. The visor fills with symbols: the HUD booting up. I breathe deep on the powdery, scorched, spicy smell of moondust. I sneeze, inhale snot, start to choke ... A golden face-plate fills my sight: Sidibe.

'Easy easy easy ...' What's she doing? A blast of cold air. I cough, hoik something warm and metallic and slimey up into my helmet. 'Easy, Emer. I've hooked you into your LSU.'

I got the helmet, I forgot the suitpack.

The thing from inside me smells of moondust, iron and stone. The drool-filters suck it up. The HUD boots up and I can see through the dust. We are here.

Wu Lock is real moon history; the original shaft drilled down into the big lava chamber of Queen of the South. I wonder what the explorers felt when they took their first step into the heart of the moon. They mapped it, measured it, hit it with radar and seismics so that they knew every rock and cranny, but mapping isn't seeing. Suit lights won't reach even a tenth of the way to the far side. Deep as space, without a single star, without the blue earth. Pure and perfect dark. Would they have thought: light has never touched this place, not even a single photon? Would they have thought: for three billion years, this place has waited in the pure and perfect dark, and once the light has touched it, it can never be the same? It's like a stain, a pollution. Thinking about that long, waiting dark made me feel funny inside, like something clenching.

Kobe waits for us in the lower lock as we cycle through out of the dust. His shell-suit's helmet is open; his head looks stupid tiny on top of the huge pile of powered armour. But he's in a shell-suit; that is the thing.

*Where do I get a shell-suit?* he'd asked.

*There are suits at Wu Lock,* I told him. *Can you make your own way there?*

*I'm Department of Transport,* he'd answered. Give Kobe a mission and he will see it through, come moonquake or meteor strike.

Beacons flash from shoulders, thighs, the small of Kobe's back. Every joint is high-contrast silver and orange. Safety first, safety last, safety always.

I run my finger through the layer of dust on one of the other shell-suits hooked into the racks. No one has used these in a long time. Maybe even since the days of the first explorers. They last forever, these things. Standing, gathering dust, waiting for someone to pop the code.

I slap Kobe on the back. Stupid. *Sore.*

'Helmet on, Kobe.' It unfolds, closes around his head. Pressure seals lock. The names and faces of my team appear over their shoulders in my augmented vision. One armoured giant, one moon-cat, Golden Girl, and Commander Cariad: we look like a superhero squad. The Fearless Four. I take status checks. Air, water, power, comms; all at full bars.

'Okay, Jair, depressurise.'

Jair lifts a clawed hand: his fingers dance among the virtual dials hovering in my augmented vision.

'Depressurising.'

My suit HUD paints the depressurisation as if I am at the bottom of a slowly draining pool of a deep green that shifts to red as it lowers. I open a private channel to Kobe.

'You all right?'

If I find the graphics spooky, it could really scare Kobe.

'This is exciting, Cariad,' Kobe answers, and his flat,

solid voice and his huge, solid bulk in the big suit seems so reasonable and right that I don't even blink as the green drains across my face, down my body in yellow to orange to seep away in swirls of red around my boots.

'Zero pressure, Cari,' Jair says.

'Open her up, Jair.' Jair touches his left wrist. New charms and magics appear in front of my eyes. A flick of Jair's claws throws them at the outer lock door. And the door splits down the middle and slides apart, like an old fairy story. Ahead of us the Wu tunnel slopes upward into a vanishing point of utter darkness. It's two small steps onto the funicular, but the shaft is long and dark and at the other end is real, solid adventure. No running out. No handing this back and saying, *No thank you not today.*

I take a deep breath.

'Team, let's go.'

———————

Up we go, me and Sidibe and Jair and Kobe, riding on a moving platform up the big, long tunnel. We have lights in the suits but we're on internal power and Sidibe's instructions are *battery first, battery last, battery always,* so we ride up to the surface by the funicular's headlights. They only shine a little way up the tunnel, which is a smooth, gently sloping tube only slightly higher than the top of Kobe's helmet with no features no details no anything to give us any clue about how fast we are moving, how far we have come or how far lies in front of us. We're wedged in the sinuses of a stone giant the size of the whole moon.

As if he has read my thoughts, Jair says, 'How much longer . . .' and before he finishes his words the red and white chevrons on the upper lock door appear in the headlights. The circular gate is ringed in flashing warning beacons. Beyond this door is the surface. Top of the world. Lady Luna. The funicular stops one short step from the lock gate.

'Okay, Jair.'

He summons his neko-magic. A ring of warning lights flash. The gate quivers, then slowly slowly parts. No one has been through the Wu Gate in a long, long time. A slot of light touches our feet, climbs our legs and bodies, shines full-bright in our faces. Our dazzle-visors cut in. The line of light widens until we are bathed in the hard glare of the floods. Beyond the light pylons the rim of Shackleton crater is a curve of hard black, deep as death. The sun rests on the upper lip of the absolute black. It rolls along that crater rim as we roll around the Earth, like it's on rails, but it never lifts more than a finger-width across the line. Blinding light and darkest shadow, next to each other. There are valleys in the lower slopes of Shackleton rim where the sun has never shone. Billion-year-old ice lies there in the darkness. We built a city on that ice. Ice and darkness and lights, the mothers of Queen of the South. Or, if you want, water, ice, and almost constant solar power. Yay, Queen! Mount Malapert is so far south, so high, it's in sunlight 340 days a year but even that's not good enough for Taiyang. The Suns want to put a tower on top of the mountain, so tall it will be in forever-sunlight. The Pavilion of Eternal Light. Seems a piece of expensive frip to me, but Laine's done work on their new big corporate headquarters at southeast Shackleton; they're calling that the Palace of Eternal Light, so I suppose there's always a clue in the name. Anyway, we are all shadows and light down at the south side of the moon. Which is my way of covering the fact that we're all frozen in the Wu Gate, dazzled and spooked by the light and the darkness.

I need to do something commanding here.

'Line up,' I say. Sidibe steps in front of me, I sense Jair and Kobe at my back. 'Let's take a walk.'

We step out of the lock, onto the surface, and walk in each other's footsteps toward the lighting pylons of Shackleton yard.

'There are sixty-four tracks in Shackleton yard,' Kobe announces. 'It's the moon's biggest rail marshaling yard. A fully robotic double hump-shunting system can compile and decompile two trains simultaneously. The northern hump sends cars of rare earths, aluminium, ores, and silicons to the big commercial airlocks. They can hold six railcars at once! The southern hump sends water, organics, renewables to the settlements along the transpolar line and the new build at Meridian.'

'Kobe, thank you,' I say. He was about to give us times and load-outs of every train between him and Rozhdestvenskiy.

'This is not pleasing,' Jair says. 'It . . . curves.'

While Kobe was info-dumping us, the rest of us were having our minds slowly stretched by the freaky bend in the world. All around my world curves away from me. The trains compiling and decompiling are so long their heads and tails are around the curve in the world. Railcars drift out of nowhere, past us, into nowhere. I had forgotten that there are things called horizons. Queen is a great bubble: from Osman Tower, dust permitting, you can see all the way to the edge of the city in any direction. You see the whole of the world. On the surface, you are on the outside of a ball. And not a very big ball at that. I feel I'm about to fall over and slide away with every step. This is Queen turned inside out. There are no walls to the world.

And then there is the Earth. The big blue. It sits where it always sits, where it sat when I was taken up to look at it: on the very edge of that crazy curved horizon, a ball balanced on another, never moving but always looking about to topple over. It is a sliver from full and I cannot take my eyes off it. None of us can.

I've heard jackaroo stories of surface workers so in love with the earthshine that they take their helmets off to see it full and clear, with nothing between them and it. Laine says that's not possible, an urban legend, but looking at the Earth, just looking at it, feeling drawn up and falling over at the same time, those legends are truer than true.

You see the blue first. Endless blue. Blue, to me, is the most terrifying colour. It is unnatural, alien, staring. Death is endless pale blue. Then you see the white on the blue—clouds: I learned that in colloq, though I still don't understand how they work. Next you see the green and brown beneath the blue—more brown than green, I'm told, and growing every year, every lune, every day. Last of all you see the lights along the night edge of the world, webs and knits and whirls of lights. I understand a terrible thing. My world, everything in it, all my friends and family, all my life, are just toys. Pretend. That is the real world: *there*.

'We should move,' Kobe says on the common channel. 'We have eight minutes thirty-seven seconds to catch our train.'

And I am back in my suit, my boots, on the dust. This little grey world is all the world we have, the only world we can have.

Kobe and Sidibe are already running out across the tracks, Jair five footfalls behind them. I turn from the liar Earth and run after them.

———

They shouldn't show you the Earth.

Look up, they say. What do you see? The thing you can never have. Up there, all blue. All shining. Can't have, can't go. The guest-workers, they can go. They have to play it right, but they can go back to that world. Us moon-born, we can never go there. Earth gravity would melt us, mash us, stop our hearts, and shatter our bones. Look up, see that? Can't have. Not yours. This is yours: rock and dust and a billion bootprints. We're shut out of heaven.

You shouldn't show us.

———

We don't have rules on the moon but we do have agreements. Some of these are contracts, some of them are more like understandings. So it's understood that any surface worker can hitch a ride on any train anywhere any time. Laine's done it hundreds of times. Gebre's never done it. He's always ridden inside, under pressure, with a seat.

I really don't know what Laine sees in him.

Kobe has tagged our train and sent the image to our helmet HUDS, a northbound freight-hauling tech and returning guest-workers to the Moonloop, water and carbon compounds to the big dig at Meridian, then calling at Hadley to stock up on metals before heading on all the way to Rozhdestvenskiy at the top of the world. Five and a half thousand kilometres. We jump the wide tracks, waiting for the silent freight cars to glide past us. Freight 1107 is like a wall across the world. The passenger bay is half a kilometre north, just behind the traction unit. We jog along the trackside. Jair tries to jump up on to the outer rail of the neighbouring track. Kobe grabs and snatches him to the ground.

'That's the power track!' Kobe yells on the common channel. 'Fifty kay volts!'

I was just about to put my boot on it.

Jair's purple and pink neko pattern is smudged black with moondust. We are all pretty dusty by now, boots and lower legs. It's a good look.

Kobe's tag leads us to the passenger bay.

'We're riding two and a half thousand kay on that?'

Jair says. He's still pissy after Kobe saved him from smoking death, but I see his point. Freight 1107's passenger accommodation is an open mesh platform, five sets of safety harnesses and life-support plugs.

'You want loungers and tea?' Sidibe says. 'This is an adventure.'

'The train departs in fifty-four seconds,' Kobe said. We swing up onto the platform and hook suitpacks and helmet comms into the sockets. Kobe counts us down from ten. The platform quivers as the maglev powers up. We are floating on magnetic fields.

'We should stand by for . . .' Kobe says. And *whoa*! Acceleration throws me across the platform. I'm looking down between cars at speed and death. Sidibe grabs one arm, Kobe the other; together they haul me back. Jair snaps the safety harness to me.

'Okay, new directive: everyone straps in,' I say, but I can hear the shake in my voice and we all know I almost died there. The train accelerates hard. We brace to keep ourselves upright. I feel the webbing of my safety harness strain.

'Six gees,' Kobe hisses. 'One Earth gravity.'

And the acceleration ends. We all lurch the opposite direction. My stomach stays where it was.

'We are travelling at one thousand kilometres per hour,' Kobe says. His voice changes. 'Oh. My stomach doesn't feel so good.' His voice breaks into a bubbling choking gasping.

'Shit, he's thrown up in his helmet,' Sidibe says.

'What do we do, what do we do?' Jair shrieks, which is the thing not to do because everyone has heard about how you can suffocate on your own vom inside a helmet.

'He's under gravity so he won't choke,' Sidibe says. 'But he is lip deep in vom. Kobe, listen, you have to open your collar seal, then the seals all the way down and let it drain. It's all right, you won't depressurise.'

Kobe burbles. Jair takes his big plastic hand in neko-paw.

'It'll be all right, Kobe.'

'The control is HUD sector 2,' Sidibe says. 'Blink up the suit interior seals menu. Got it?'

Kobe grunts. Jair squeezes his hand, as much as a tight-weave bodyskin can squeeze armoured plastic.

'Make it so, Kobe.'

A different grunt.

'So, you'll be walking around in chuck, but that's better than being up to the chin in it,' Sidibe says.

'How do you know this?' I asked.

'My ex-iz was a VTO track queen,' Sidibe says.

'I'm not feeling great now either,' Jair says. Truth, I feel kind of vommy too. It's like kids in colloq, one starts, everyone follows. I try not to think about the vom trickling down Kobe's body, pooling in his boots. Looking out at the surface-scape, that's what makes the gut lurches. Out there is a blinding blur. Crater? Building? Machine? Mountain? Blink blink blink blink blink. A train passes in a blink of light. I think I screamed. If I did, I hope it wasn't on the common channel.

'I've an idea,' I say. 'Don't look at anything. You'll get motion sick. Shut down your visor and play a game or watch a telenovela.'

'I like looking,' Sidibe says. 'It's exciting.' She's right at the edge of the platform, clinging to the rail with one hand, peering ahead up the train. Just looking at her my stomach goes again.

'Well, you enjoy it,' I say and polarise my helmet. I play Run the Jewels until my mind is ragged. I try to talk to Jair, but comms show he's on a private channel with Kobe so I switch to old runs of *Lansberg Crater*. Even at a thousand kilometres per hour, two and a half thousand kays is a lot of telenovela.

VTO trains run to the millisecond, so Kobe can count us down to deceleration. It's still pretty savage. We brace, we put out our arms to stop us slamming into the bulkhead, we grit our teeth and plant our feet and wrestle gravity as the big train comes to a halt.

We open our eyes, we depolarise our helmets.

Meridian. Centre of the world.

———————

So, Earth has these things called icebergs. They float on oceans and they're big, but the thing is, because of density, the *really* big is under the surface. Our cities are like that. You see a solar array, comms towers, locks and docking bays, lots and lots of old machinery and piled regolith, the BALTRAN, the railroad lines, maybe the Moonloop. And you think, that's impressive, but the real city, the big city, is under the surface.

When it's finished, Meridian will be the largest city on the moon. They're building for three million people. We're not even a tenth of that right now, but we're always future-facing. So Laine tells me. Meridian says, *Humans are on the moon to stay.*

Kobe explains to me why the name 'Meridian.' It's where the equator and the zero north-south lines meet. The closest point to Earth. Our major spaceport. Because there's all this surface junk and then there is the Moonloop tower. Two kilometres of girders and elevators and if you crank up the magnification on your HUD, you can see the transfer platform at the top. Crank up another notch and you make out the capsules. Tether orbits are known down to the millisecond so you can watch the grapple-end of a tether spin down from orbit, latch with the capsule, and snatch it up and away. At any time, hundreds of cargo capsules are flying between moon and Earth. Trade between worlds, like a weird, lovely dance. The Moonloop has never failed to catch an incoming capsule. Never. The tethers are too thin to be seen, even under full HUD magnification, so it looks as if the capsule suddenly decides to shoot up and forwards into the big black. It's one of those things you could watch all day: the railcars offloading capsules, the cargoes going up and down the elevator and vanishing up into space.

But that's not what I'm staring at. Oh no. That evil blue Earth? Down south, she sits on the edge of the Shackleton, like something waiting to eat you. Up here at the centre of the world she's at the top of the sky, right overhead. That sure tells you that you've come halfway around the world in a couple of hours, and that makes you feel big and small at the same time.

'You want to get thrown up into orbit?' Sidibe says. I realise I'm staring.

'Our car will rendezvous with the Moonloop in thirty-three seconds,' Kobe says. 'We should exit before then.'

'Team: let's walk,' I say, and one by one we drop to the regolith. My HUD shows me a cluster of old accommodation tubes and a lock. 'With me.' And it's like the connection with the regolith grounds me, and I feel a shock run through me—not static—but the realisation, among these buildings and trains and towers with the Earth high above me, that I am a very, very long way from home.

'Come on, Kobe, I'll find you a banya,' Jair says. He takes Kobe's hand. 'We'll get you cleaned up.'

---

I don't think it's defensive. I don't think it's defensive at all.

Right, so: maybe *that* is, but telling it like a story, why should that be defensive? Understand: it's my language. It's how I tell things: stories. Narratives. No, narratives aren't false. They're just differently true. You have to be able to read them, read into them, read under them. If I tell this as a story, why should you think it's any less of the truth than if I had some emotional breakdown and pissed everything out onto this kind of nice chair? I didn't ask to be here. I certainly didn't ask for an AI. There has to be a deal: there has to be a deal in everything. It's how we live. You get the truth, but you get it my way. You haven't got a right to it. You have to negotiate it.

So: you listen to my story. And anyway, what's wrong with defending yourself?

---

Even I, Captain Cariad, am rocked back by Meridian. The

inlock opens and we walk along a tunnel to an elevator down to a ramp that takes us onto a shelf at the top of a canyon half a kilometre wide, three kilometres high, and so long I can't see the end of it, just dim dusty grey that hints at other canyons beyond my seeing. Shafts of light from a thousand lighting arrays stab through the dusty air; drones skip and buzz all around us. Cranes swing over our heads; cranes above cranes above cranes. My jaw is like, *A-whuh?* The noise is deafening: excavators, constructors, sealers, sinterers, and smelters. It's like being inside God's voice-box. This is real city-building.

Sidibe unseals her helmet, shakes out her fabulous hair. Her eyes are wide and full of wonder.

'Imagine flying in here,' she says. 'You'd never come down.'

I remove my helmet and breathe in the dust and electric air.

'Um, guys?' Jair takes his helmet off and shouts over the racket. 'Kobe says, sorry he hasn't opened his helmet yet, but he's ankle deep in vom?'

———

So Jair walks us past the Sultan Imperial, and the Rus and the Yellow Moon and even this construction-worker banya with no name only a silver tree lasered into the stone door until I remind him that he was the one who reminded *us* that Kobe was up to the ankles in three-hour-old stomach contents.

'Not private enough,' Jair says, hunching over to make himself look smaller, which he does when he feels self-conscious.

'Oh, for gods' sake,' Sidibe says, holding her helmet up to her face to blink a few instructions to her HUD. 'Your ceegee's credit still good?'

Jair nods, frowning.

'Then follow me.'

She leads us up along a half-made street excavated from the side of the canyon, down three ramps and two access gantries and half a kilometre along another, lower, wall-hugging street to a service bridge leaping half a kilometre across the gulf.

'Well, come on, then.'

'On that?' Jair says. I'm glad he does. It means I don't have to.

'Bots use them all the time,' Sidibe says. She steps onto the bridge. It's an arch of construction beams with aluminium mesh spot-fused to the flat side. It's the width of my suitpack. This is sweet for you, flying girl. You throw yourself off the tops of tall towers. Cariad Corcoran's inner bits are still woozy from the train ride. Kobe steps after her; they march confidently across the bridge.

'Hey!' Jair darts in behind them. So what if heights don't faze you, you with your high and broody neko-roosts all over Osman Tower? It's the fact that you're scared to get naked around strangers got us here in the first place. If I wait any longer they'll be too far ahead of me. I step out onto the mesh. Don't look down. I focus on the silver and orange helmet seal on Kobe's suit. And yes, the bridge springs as we march in single file. One foot in front of the other, Cariad. Don't look down. Silver and orange. Silver and orange.

I feel ready to risk a joke.

'Hey Sidibe, what happens if we meet a . . .'

Bot. Turning off the roadway ahead of us, onto a bridge. A big bot, wide as a buddha, as many arms as a god.

'Stop stop stop!' I shout. The machine steps onto the bridge. It marches towards us, at the very centre of the span.

'Back up!' Sidibe yells.

'I can't!' I shout. I can't back up. Impossible, impossible, can't you see that's a stupid thing to say, Sidibe Sisay?

'Then turn around!' Sidibe yells, but I can't do that either. I can't do anything, can't move a foot because if I make one move, however small, I will fall.

'Make it go back!' I shout, but the bot strides towards us, one step two step three step four. Boom boom boom and the bridge is really bouncing now and there is nothing to hold on to and the bot isn't stopping and its four steps three steps two steps and Jair is shouting that Kobe is saying something and at the last moment the bot swings itself upside down to cling underneath the bridge and in a scurry of way too many legs passes beneath us. I hear, I feel its too-many feet click and tap on the metal.

I try to breathe. I fix on Kobe's neck seal Kobe's neck seal Kobe's neck seal and I find myself exhaling a breath that I have held for, I think, a very long time.

'Everyone all right?' Sidibe says.

'Kobe says the bots are coded to avoid humans,' Jair says, and the big hulk-monster nods its helmet. 'For safety.'

'Let's go,' Sidibe says, and I say nothing and put one foot in front of another in front of another until I am off this bridge.

Three levels down we pile into the lobby of the Han Ying Hotel. I'm still shaking, but together enough to notice that I'm in a high-status establishment. It's a new place, for managerial and executive and Lunar Development Corporation guanlis—anyone who doesn't have or doesn't want a berth in one of the workers' hostels. Because it's classy, there's a human on the desk who smiles as he takes Jair's bio-mom's credit authorisation, whose smile freezes when he spies the dusty footprints we've left across his freshly carpeted lobby. Classy enough for him to say not one word, key our thumbs to the locks, and summon the cleaning bots as we head up the stairs to our suite. Classy indeed, but this is true class: every suite has a private banya.

Jair drags a sheet off the bed as we peel off sasuits. Kobe pops the shell-suit.

We leap back. We leap so far back we hit the bedroom wall. Not even death could smell that bad. My stomach lifts. Jair has wrapped his sheet across his face. I snatch up hand towels, one for me, one for Sidibe, and we follow Jair's inspiration. Somehow we get Kobe into the shower. It takes three cycles before we let him join us in the hot pool.

We spread our arms out along the edge of the pool and very, very slowly start to feel like heroes. A quarter the way round the world clinging to a high-speed freighter. Facing down killer bots on the Bridge of Forever. There are dusters and jackaroos and VTO track queens who would salute anyone for that. Let alone us.

'How do you feel, Kobe?' Jair asks. Jair has somehow done something amazing with his hair so he can look out from under it again.

'The smell is still up my nose,' Kobe says.

'Emer.'

For a moment I am so lapped and loved in neck-deep ooh-warm water I don't recognise the name.

Emer. Is me. Can only be Sidibe.

'We kind of need to . . . clean out Kobe's suit,' she says. My heart shrinks.

'In good time, in good time,' I say. Jesus and Mary, I sound like Laine. 'Can we not just stay here for a while longer?'

'Um, Cari,' Jair says, and his legs are pulled into his chest and he is resting his chin on his knees, which is not a good thing. 'We probably shouldn't stay here too long? Sooner or later Dolores is going to notice what's been happening to her account.'

Shit. No, not shit. *Shite.*

'Right, then, we clean out Kobe's suit. In relays, one at a time. Jair, get the rover. Okay. Sidibe, you're first.'

Sidibe bares her teeth at me—her teeth! Such insubordination!—and grabs a handful of paper towels as she scoots wet foot and bare ass across the stone to Kobe's vom-crusted shell-suit. I sink into the warm water and let it flow up my arms, around my neck, feel my hair floating out in the bubbles, and for a few moments I am in love with everyone, my team, my jackaroos, even Sidibe. Vom will come, in time. Vom always comes. But for this moment I am Cariad Corcoran, explorer. In her pool in a hole in a suite in a hotel in the moon.

'That's the rover?'

This is one time I'm happy Sidibe is a syllable ahead of me. We are suited and booted and rosy-fresh scented and Jair has just worked his kitty-magic with Dolores's authorisation. If Wu Lock in Queen was like being squeezed out of the birth canal, Meridian's Great Eastern Lock is like the bio-mother of all handball arenas. Right, so, those metaphors don't exactly work together, but they make their point. You can see them, right? That's all you need. What I mean is, Wu was small; this one is so big we look like stones shaken off someone's boots in all the polished rock. There are vehicle bays in the walls, protected by long strips of dust-netting. Kobe tells us one day they will put spaceships in here. Not spaceships. *Moon*ships. What big really means is that we have a lot of space and time to study the machine that comes scurrying out from behind the dust sheeting and slides to a halt in front of us.

'I was expecting *windows,*' I say. Windows, environment pod, comfort. '*Pressurisation.*'

'The VTO588 line has never been pressurised,' Kobe says.

'Jair, get us a pressurised rover,' I said.

'Dolores doesn't have the access.'

'She had access to a suite at the Han Ying Hotel,' Sidibe says.

'She had money for the suite at the Han Ying Hotel,' Jair says, and for the first time do I hear a little edge of irritation with Sidibe? This is something I can use, an edge I can lift and tear back. Like that time Kobe fell asleep in the light-bath and he blistered and I peeled the bubbled skin off his back in big, stretchy, satisfying sheets. Understand: only because he couldn't do it himself. Only because the itching was driving him insane. 'This is an access thing. Her company isn't contracted for full-environment rovers.'

'We'll take it,' I say. We need to get out of this city, out to where no one can stop us. Off the network. Wild and free, my adventurers!

Jair circles a finger in the air and the rover runs up to us, cute as a baby ferret, and lifts its safety bars. Four seats, open to vacuum, facing outwards, on either side of a power and life-support truss. Big wheels, taller than Jair. Batteries and comms arrays. Cables and pipes and conduits and trucking and struts: everyone exposed and open. Bare naked.

'Where does the driver sit?' I ask.

'The VTO588 doesn't have a driver as such,' Kobe says. 'It's a fully autonomous surface rover, though any passenger may assume control of the control HUD.'

'It needs a . . . captain,' I say.

'The VTO588 is a fully autonomous surface rover,' Kobe says again.

'It needs a name,' Sidibe cuts in.

'The VTO588 does not require a name,' Kobe announces. 'That's kind of anthropomorphist.'

'Don't care. I'm going to call it Redrover,' Sidibe says and hop-spins up and round to slap her goldy-looking ass into the front right seat.

*I am happy to respond to whatever form of address you decide,* says a voice from nowhere on the common channel.

'Redrover?' Sidibe says, and the voice—like an eight-year-old—says *yes* and the rover flashes its lights. It has a lot of lights. Right, so: we're in danger of dicking around in the lock until the ceegees shut off our credit or our air runs out. This is why there has to be a captain.

'Everyone aboard,' I order. I'm sure to get the front left seat. Jair slips in behind me. Sidibe has Mount Kobe to her right. We seal helmets and follow the on-HUD instructions to hook up our life-support and comms. Safety bars descend and lock.

'Everyone ready?'

My display reads four greens.

'Redrover, take us out,' I order.

Redrover sits dead still on the long gentle ramp of

Meridian Great Eastern outlock. Not a twitch, not even a hum of motor.

'Redrover, take us out,' I say again.

'Um, the person giving the commands?' Jair says. 'It has to be the person on the contract. And that's, um. Me.'

Shit on this. Have I somehow dicked-off Lady Luna? No, her irritation would be a lot more drawn out. And final.

'Take us out, Mr Santa-ana,' I say.

And still still still we sit.

'Cariad,' Jair says, 'Redrover needs a destination.'

I flash the numbers to Jair.

'Now can we go?'

And I feel Redrover come alive around me. Engines hum, comms dishes rise from sleep, all those lights flick to life. Information floods onto my HUD—maps, schematics, readouts. The acceleration is nowhere near as powerful as the big maglev transpolar express, but because I am connected to it physically, intimately, by every sense, it's so so so thrilling. I can feel power in every joint and muscle, in my lungs, in my pee bladder, in my vag.

Redrover surges forward; the big wheels spin right by my head, I can feel every crack and pebble in the rock floor through the suspension and we are racing up the big long slope to the slowly widening slot of darkness—it's too slow, it's won't be open wide enough, we'll not get through. I hold my breath and Redrover hurtles out. We come off the edge of the ramp at ludicrous speed and we are flying. We hit regolith with a crack that loosens every tooth in my head, every vertebra in my spine; we bounce, hit again with a jolt that sends stars through my brain and *we are still accelerating*!

I hook my fingers around the crash bars, blink off the comms, and squeal, just squeal! as Redrover burns across the Sinus Medii. One hundred and fifty, one hundred and eighty kilometres per hour! Our dust plume must be visible from orbit. Sidibe blinks up on my HUD. I open a channel. She can barely push the words past the shaking and jolting as Redrover takes the smaller rocks and stones and dodges the big, wrecking ones.

'This. Is. Fantastic!'

It is fantastic. This, *this,* is Adventure.

We ride the craters, the sudden lurch as we roll down over the rim—don't lose your lunch, Kobe! (Kobe's lunch was grazing through the snack dispenser at the Han Ying. Everyone's lunch was grazing through the snack dispenser at the Han Ying: I haven't given as much thought to logistics as I probably should—in fact, I haven't given any thought.) Then we come up the far rim and fly up far and high and bang down in explosions of dust and clanging suspension.

I admit it: it wouldn't have been anywhere near as

much fun in a pressurised rover.

Then I feel a sharp crack through the metal. In the side of my eye I see Jair's head snap to one side. My HUD fills with red warnings.

'Stop stop stop,' I shout, but Redrover can't hear me. Jair has the word for the rover, and in my helmet Jair's suit integrity is dropping fast into the white.

Every kid on the moon knows what white means: death.

'Make it stop!' I shout. Then I hear Kobe's voice on the common channel.

'Redrover, medical emergency control.'

*Medical emergency identified. You have control.*

'Stop and release, Redrover.'

And Redrover stops. And Redrover lifts the crash bars and lowers the seat and I drop to the regolith but Sidibe is already kneeling in front of Jair. He isn't speaking. He isn't responding. And his visor is starred with cracks, and my HUD is insane with alerts and I don't know what to do.

'A stone must have flown up and hit his helmet,' Sidibe says. 'He's leaking atmosphere. Not good. Not good.'

'What can we do, what can we do?' I say. I am dodging from one foot to another, my little panic dance. From adventure to Jesus and Mary. In the blinking of an eye.

'Model 588s carry suit-repair kits at each seating station,' Kobe says from around the rover. Redrover outlines a hatch next to Jair's head. I reach for it, Sidibe slaps my hand away.

'Don't touch what you don't understand.'

The panel pops out, Sidibe removes a spray tube the size of my suited-up thumb. She twists off the cap, shakes it, and carefully works over the cracks. The sealant is precise, Sidibe is slow and careful, and inside my helmet the white climbs to red to green.

'Jair?'

Grunts and murmurs on the common channel.

'You okay?'

Sidibe throws the empty can far out across the Sinus Medii.

'I'm okay.'

'That'll hold it,' Sidibe says. 'That stuff is stronger than the thing it fixes. You might have a problem seeing out of the right side of your visor.'

'I'm okay.'

'Emer, is he okay?'

There is too much Jair on my visor, but from what I can read, he is green green green.

'He's good to go.'

'I'm okay.'

I must make a command decision.

'Kobe, you have control of Redrover?'

'Through the medical emergency override, yes.'

'I think you should drive.'

'I'll only have it until Redrover identifies the medical emergency as over.'

'Then it'll go back to Jair?'

'Yes.'

'All good, then. Okay, team, seat up and move out.'

---

Why should it be interesting that I wanted to be captain? Someone needed to be.

Collective decisioning? With four folk like Kobe, Jair, Sidibe, and me? Do you want me to count off the neuro- and socio-atypicalities on my fingers? It would have been like one of those RPGs: everyone talks around and around for an hour before anyone can decide on doing anything. I prepare a Charm of Investigation. Or my Warding of Safekeeping? I summon my Mystic Armour of Total Hardness ... hang on ... no ... maybe my Suit of Lithe Leaping. Oh, I don't know. I ready a Casting of Level 12 Stinky-Fart—oh, I suppose a Level 28 Lighting Storm would be more sure-fire, but it's not as much fun ... Yadda yadda yadda.

Understand, I was just moving the indoors order of things outdoors. Laine's away a lot, Dolores is evil, Andros is gone, and someone has to keep the boys ship-shape and sweet-smelling. Me. Cariad Corcoran. I know how Kobe works, and Jair, well, he doesn't know what he doesn't know. I do. They need looking after. They need a captain.

We needed a captain.

Anyway, it's not me who makes the decision, up there. Lady Luna makes it for you.

———

Understand this: the moon at 180 kilometres an hour is fast, fun, and dangerous.

The moon at eighty kilometres an hour is slow, safe, and boring. That's the speed of a medical emergency override. So as not to shake the patient up too much. Even when Redrover decides Jair is fit and ready to take control again (which is many kilometres after Jair decides he's fit and ready to take control), we trundle along at Safe. Sane. Speed.

Next flying stone might not be so lucky.

But you have to do something to make that slow time pass, to make the boring fun. And if you can't drive dangerous, then you have to talk dangerous.

I blame Sidibe. Right, so, I would blame Sidibe, but I also blame myself, too, a little. I have to ask her how she learned the trick with the fix-spray.

'That would be the time I was out with Geetanjali at Spitzbergen Mountain,' Sidibe says.

'Geetanjali?' Jair asks. My machines tell me in a hundred different ways he's all right, no harm done, but I know Jair, and this is one uncharacteristically quiet neko. He's hardly spoken two words since Kobe sent Redrover out again.

'My ceegee,' Sidibe says. 'Before Gebre.'

We're rolling along the well-worn track beside the new-build equatorial railway, all polite and good. Next year, we could ride the Equatorial Express right to the research facility at Hypatia and walk to the Armstrong Footprint. But that's not an Adventure. That would be as far from Adventure as I can imagine. That would be tourism. 'We were an hour out of Archimedes in a selenological survey rover. Prospecting Spitzbergen for rare earths. I was eight but I can still remember it so sharp.'

'You were eight?' I said.

'So?'

'You were eight and Geetanjali took you prospecting on the Sea of Rains in a rover?'

'Pressurised,' Sidibe said. That wasn't the point, but neither was this my story. 'If there had been anyone she could have left me with she would have, but this was long before Gebre. Anyway, there we were. Stone stone stone stone crater, stone stone stone stone mountain! And then there was a flash of light in my head and in the middle of the viewing port there was a tiny white mark. Tiny, but it went through the glass outside to inside and I don't need to tell you, but rover glass is thick. Geets said, did you see that, so she had seen the flash too and I went to get a good close look at the white mark in the window but Geets pushed me away and as she did I heard this noise like a million tiny things breaking and in an instant the whole window was nothing but cracks.'

'In a pressurised rover,' Kobe says.

'It could have blown at any time,' Sidibe says. 'The slightest jolt, the tiniest rock under one of our wheels, could have done it. And we would have been . . .' She makes a whistley-explodey noise.

'What did you do?' Jair asks.

'Well, survived,' I say. 'Obviously.'

'Cariad, I want to hear this,' Kobe says.

'Geets knew that all rovers have emergency sealant,' Sidibe says. 'But it was on the rover's skin, so she had to suit up and lock through and do it from the outside. She had to work so so slowly, so so carefully, because if she put the slightest pressure on the window, it would shatter. And she was wearing the only suit.' Sidibe gives us all a storyteller's second. 'The only suit.'

'She fixed it,' I says. 'Obviously.'

'Obviously,' Sidibe says. 'But when we got back to Archimedes the lock-boss took one look at the rover and said, you owe someone. You should be dead.'

'What did it?' Kobe asks. 'Made the white crack?'

'The lock-boss reckoned it was a cosmic ray strike. Some particle kicked up to super-charge by, like, neutron stars colliding. Travels for half of forever across the universe and ends bang in our view port. That was the flash, you see? It must have gone straight through the port, Geetanjali, and me.'

'That's the scary bit,' I say. 'A cosmic ray from the dawn of time went right through your brain.'

Jair butts in. 'The scary bit is how many have gone through us since we got up on the train; how many are going through us right now.'

'Eight lunes later, Geets got sick with cancer,' Sidibe says. 'That's how I moved in with Gebre.'

'What happened to her?' I ask.

'She died,' Sidibe says. That bums us all into a long quiet, not thinking about the millions billions trillions of things shooting through us as we sit strapped in our seats merrily rolling along in Redrover. But it has given us our fun game to make the time pass quickly: what's the scariest thing ever happened to you?

———————

'I heard it long before I saw it.'

Now it's Kobe's turn to tell us the scariest thing ever happened to him. And that is a way to start a scare-story.

'Because what I heard, I didn't want to see.'

And that is the way to follow your scary story through.

'I was asleep, in my room. It was late.'

I know this story, I was asleep in the next room and I heard the noise and I saw the thing and I helped chase it out. This all happened about eight lunes ago. It's scary-fresh. Kobe has to have a little bio-light, a little glow by his head, to be able to sleep. Dark scares him. But this thing he heard; it wasn't afraid of the light. It was bigger, bolder, braver than the things that crawled only in the dark.

'It made this noise,' Kobe says, and somehow a sound comes out of him that is so uncanny, so un-Kobe, that it makes me shiver right into the marrow of my backbone; and I know the story. One moment there's his slow, careful voice, then there's this fluttering, rattling, wheezing sound that seems to have no connection with anything human. 'It . . . it was in the room with me, moving around above me.' Again he makes the noise. Sidibe and Jair do not say a word. We're suited up on the outside of a rover rolling beside the railroad track towards West Tranquility, hard vacuum and hard radiation out there, and we are scared stupid. By a silly little noise.

And I know the story . . .

'I pulled the sheet over my head,' Kobe says, and I am there, with him, with his nightlight turning it to a glowing tent of fabric. 'But I could still hear it moving around above.' Flutter flutter flutter. 'Sometimes high, sometimes low. Then all of a sudden it was real loud and I saw a shadow flash across on the sheet. Flash! And I yelled and threw back the sheet and it flew up right up and away from me and I scared it because it was just flying around and around and I couldn't get away from all the flappiness and noise and not knowing what it was going to do next.'

'What was it?' Sidibe asks.

'A bird.'

'A bird?'

'A ring-neck parakeet,' I say. 'There's a small feral population in Queen.'

'All I saw was flapping wings and all this sudden dartiness and that was really scary,' Kobe says. He needs to have things worked out, to have a plan. He can't deal with the unpredictable, the flappy.

'What happened?' Sidibe asks.

'I started screaming,' Kobe says. That was the first time I heard his fear scream, which is like nothing that could possibly come out of a human mouth. 'It just made the bird worse.'

'I came to help,' I say.

'Cariad came,' Kobe says. 'And Laine. They put out all the lights in the room and went onto the balcony with a bio-light and lured it out.

'It flew away.' I say. 'There's a couple of pairs up on the top of the tower. Folk feed them. This one must have come in through the balcony and got trapped. Kobe likes fresh air.'

'I didn't know what I was,' Kobe says. 'I didn't know there was such a thing as a bird. I'd never seen one. Everything was wrong with it. Living and flying? That thing on its face, and the feet? Flapping, those long beaty things . . .'

'Wings,' Jair says.

'Feathers,' I say. 'It had shed a bit. Kobe had to move in with me until we got the room sterilised.'

'I might catch something from them,' Kobe says, and I can hear the disgust still in his voice. 'Birds are wrong.'

He's right, though. Birds are the wrongest wrong.

We're quiet for a while, rolling along respectable beside the rail track, imagining the terror of something totally unknown in your room with you. Because it wasn't a ring-neck parakeet, it wasn't a bird, it was the most alien alien.

'I've got a story,' Jair says after a time. 'If you want to hear it.'

'I would like to hear that, Jair,' Kobe says.

'It was the last time I saw a dead person,' Jair begins in a voice so low and soft it's like licking my ear.

---

The moon wants to kill you and knows a thousand ways to do it.

We've all seen dead people. Maybe we've even seen people die. I have, says Jair, for this is his scare story. My abuelo-izquierda Huw got cancer. He was one of the early settlers. He came up with Robert Mackenzie. No one really knew what it was like here then. The radiation was chipping away at him for years. I say cancer, but it was like cancers. All everywhere. So maybe it wasn't cancers but he was one big cancer, all of him. I was there when the medics came from the dignity house. We were all there. It was happy; he was in a lot of pain and really old and we all just wanted the best for Abuelo Huw. He wouldn't let a bot do it. He wanted someone to look into his eyes.

I looked into his eyes afterwards. What I couldn't work out was, what was different? It was the same cells, the same liquids and everything, so why was Huw alive ten minutes ago and dead now? Strange.

That wasn't the scary thing.

My three-iz, Oleg, he was a zabbaleen.

Have you ever met a zabbaleen? Didn't think so. Everyone knows about them; no one ever meets them. But they're real people. You can be related to them. I was, until it all moved around again. Oleg was a zabbaleen. And he was not a nice person. He was a piss-drip. Dick-wipe. Not a good man. For a start, he was way older. And he liked to try and surprise people, shock them, get some reaction off them.

He said to me, Do you ever wonder what happens to them after they're dead?

I said: You take them.

And he said: That's smart, but after we take them, what happens?

And I said, Everything gets recycled.

He said, Would you like to see what really happens?

And I said, Abuelo Huw?

No no no, he said. That would be disrespectful. Some-one else.

So I said yes. I don't know why I said yes. I knew it would be vile: that's Oleg being Oleg. But I said yes. I wanted there to be more than just a person on a bed, dead. I wanted there to be more than just me, with Abuelo Huw, and maybe I'd kiss him or touch him or just say something to him, and then I would walk out of the room and there would be nothing of him ever again. Maybe it was he was the first person I ever saw die and I was still just messed around because I couldn't take in what happened.

But I said yes.

There's a whole other world, in there. Inside Queen. Inside every city. It's like the veins and arteries in your body; that takes all the stuff around you but you never see it. In every building, under every street, there are doors and entrances and hidden tunnels and the zab-baleen come out, do their work, disappear again, and you never know. You never see. They don't want to be seen. They want it to be like a trick. But they make everything work.

So I met Oleg in the lobby of Kingscourt Tower and he opened a bit of the wall I didn't know could open and we stepped through and we were in this corridor, right beside the lobby, right beside all the things and people I saw every day. I could hear them, I could see them through the cameras. And they didn't know I was there, right beside them.

Oleg took me down to the tunnel. They have tunnels, and roads, and jitneys. They got to move a lot of stuff around real discreet. I got to ride with Oleg in one of the jitneys, right under the boulevards, around the roots of the towers, where all the pipes and cables and trunking goes.

The place where they recycle the bodies is at the very middle of Queen, right under the Taiyang Tower. Oleg said they had their own name for it, but he couldn't tell me because it was a zabbaleen secret. I think it was because it was some bad taste joke. Professionals make jokes like that, that are just for them.

First place Oleg took me was the de-sleeving room.

Do you know what de-sleeving is?

I'll tell you. It's removing the skin. Before you can get to anything else, you have to get the wrapper off.

Do you want to see it, Oleg asked. And then I really saw where I was and I said, No, oh no, gods no, and Oleg shrugged and said, Well, we'll move along then.

The skin. They take the skin off. One piece. Peeled off.

Oleg took me to another room and said, This is where we get the bones out. Best bit of the human body, the bones. Bones and teeth. We're a calcium-deficient population. Don't suppose you want to see that either, and no I did not, and I did not want to see the tanks where they sloosh in what's left when they take the bones out and enzymes dissolves it all to goop, and where they separate out the chemicals from the goop and the room where they compost the bits they can reprocess and the audit office where they measure and weigh all the chemicals and give you an account: calcium this, carbon that, phosphorous other. I didn't want to see any of it, I didn't want to be there, I wished I'd never gone, because I could see, in my mind; I could see Huw on the table and the machines going in and unpeeling him like a banana.

Down there, that place, that was the most scared I ever was. Because there's dead, and I understand that, it's the thing that wakes me up in the night, out there, perching on my balcony, never going away, but after death: there's that. And that will happen to every single one of us. No escape, no exemptions. If the zabbaleen are anything, they are thorough. Even if we died out here, however long it took to find whatever the moon left of us, the zabbaleen would take it back to their deep rooms, and take it all to pieces.

And I know, in my head, that I'm dead, what do I care, it's natural and right that I return everything I borrowed back to the moon again. It's that it will happen to everyone you ever know, you ever love. Your ceegees, your friends. If you ever marry, in or out of the ring: them too. You Kobe, you Cari, you Sidibe. I see you on that table, the skin peeled back from your face. I see your bones cut out of your body. I see you sliding down that chute into the big enzyme bath.

And that scares me.

———————

'Jesus Joseph and Mary, Jair,' I say on the common channel.

'You asked me,' Jair says. 'I told you.'

'Kobe?' Sidibe's voice. 'Are you all right?'

There is a silence so long I check Kobe's suit read-outs on my HUD. Green spiking into yellow. Anxiety, fight-or-flight reactions.

'Is this true?' Kobe asks.

'Truest thing . . .' Jair starts, and there is a hardness, an edge like black moon obsidian in his voice that I have never heard before and never suspected from my neko boy.

'I'm scared,' Kobe says, and I hear fear in his voice, the fear that can't move and can't breathe.

'No more scare stories,' I say. "That's an Executive Order.'

'Just before you have to tell yours,' Jair says, but he shuts up and I see on my HUD that Sidibe and Kobe have a private channel open. I try to listen in—Executive Privilege—but I don't have the access code and anyway at that moment a blip appears on my map. Theon Habitat.

Which is a good thing, because in all our excitement at getting to Meridian, getting the rover, getting out onto the surface, getting on our way to adventure, we forgot to pack any food.

And who is Department of Surface Activity, Sidibe Sisay?

----------

So, as my story takes a natural break while we load up food, I'm going to talk to you about Jair. I'm going to tell you exactly how it is because I don't want you putting your theory on him. I don't want you stroking your beard, which you don't have, or your chin which you even more don't have and thinking, mm, Thanatos death force; aha, Eros life force.

Understand: ring marriages are not just complicated, they are more complicated than you can know. Not everyone-you. You-you. You can pull up all the data you like, but you will never know it, truly, because you have to be in one to know one. So, I can't speak for other rings, in Oruka Ring, no one has ever married an AI. Yet.

Yes, I know 'Oruka' is Yoruba for ring. Ring-ring. Your point?

So, it's a tautology. I will try and help you understand.

Jair is: the cutest neko in the Queen of the South. Jair was: the cutest kid this side of the ring. Jair has always been: my iz. Jair's ceegee, Dolores, is also his bio-mom, but she engineers things and so she's been on one build or another for most of his boy-and-neko-hood. So she asked Laine to be his primary ceegee and now he lives with us. Laine also engineers things and she's away a lot, but somehow that's not a problem to Dolores.

I've said that I will never understand what Laine sees in Dolores?

Jair hardly ever goes back to Dolores now. Why couldn't it have been her crossed the ring?

So what if I've said that before? Yes, it's significant.

I see what you're doing there. Asking me why I think that Jair is cute. I don't *think* Jair is cute. I said Jair *is* cute. I said it because it's an objective fact, like Cariad Corcoran has red hair and freckles. Jair is cute. The moon goes round the Earth. It's the way of things. Yes. Really.

---

Whoever named Theon a habitat has either (a) never been there or (b) a sick, sick sense of humour. Actually, maybe both. Theon is nothing more than a half-pipe of corrugated aluminium with an airlock at one end, bermed over with regolith to keep some of the radiation at bay. My room back at Osman Tower is more spacious and welcoming. This will be as intimate as a banya. At least we can keep our clothes on, and take our helmets off. Oh Holy Family, I can't wait to do that. I'm starting to get the twitches about this curve of visor Right. In. Front. Of. My. Face.

By Old Tradition, humpies and habitats are open to anyone who needs one, so no need for Jair's magic. I send him through the lock first, in case there's something inside that does need a touch of the neko-paw; then Kobe. He fills the entire chamber in his big bright Peril Suit.

'Sid.'

She hates that.

'I need to talk to you.'

We lean against Redrover's rear right wheel. It looms over us, all struts and mesh and suspension bars. It's good to stand. Good to lean. I'm not looking forward to slapping my butt back in that seat.

'You were talking with Kobe,' I say. 'On a private channel.'

'I was.'

'Right, so,' I say. 'I'm the leader and it's not good for leadership if my team is talking behind my back.'

'I was talking privately with Kobe,' Sidibe says. 'Jair scared him.'

Jair scared us all, but I'm not going to tell her that.

'I could have talked to Kobe. I know him.'

'Not on an open channel.'

'What?'

'He would never have talked on an open channel. Not with you on it, Emer. Kobe has a role he plays with you. He doesn't have one with me. So he can talk.'

'Are you saying you know Kobe better than me?'

'I'm saying there are things he says to you and there are things he won't say to you. He's sensitive.'

'He has his rules and rituals, he needs to prepare for new things.'

'He needs to picture new things in his head, walk right around them, look at them from every angle before he can deal with them. What Jair said: Kobe saw that. In every detail.'

I cannot argue here. I should not argue. I need not argue. But Cariad Corcoran has to have the last word.

'Good work, Department of Surface Activity.' I tap Sidibe on the shoulder of her sasuit. 'I appoint you Department of Morale and Emotional Well-Being.' Laine worked for a while with Taiyang; that's where I learned all those flowery titles. I've always been big for smart words and flowery titles. I like the way they feel in my head, in my mouth.

I follow Sidibe through the lock into the humpie. I take my helmet off—away from me, away from me, vile visor!—take a breath of free air, and almost vom up. It's not Kobe's in-suit vom—we were strict with the cleanup, though a certain *aroma* lingers. It's us. Breathing each other in. Two hours in a suit, everything recycled over and over and over; you reek. Even the girls. We stink and we look tired and a long way from home. We *are* a long way from home. Four of us, in suits, huddled together under a roof so low the boys have to stoop, in the middle of the Trans-Medii Highlands. No one knows we're here.

'Team First Footprint!' I say big and loud. 'Here we are. Here we are!' I've heard this kind of thing in motivational talks. I'm not sure anyone ever really speaks like this, but Theon feels like an Achievement.

Even Jair raises a paw and a cheer.

The habitat AI lists the rations in the humpie's lockers. There are sucky-tubes and squeezy-tubes in a variety of Appealing Flavours. I squeeze, I suck, and my read-outs say I'm nourished even if I feel nothing in my belly. From the sour faces I guess everyone else has had the same Theon dining experience. We drink the humpie's water because, who really wants to drink suit-water? You know?

'We good, team?' I say. The response is a little half-hearted. Two and some hours in the rover to get to Tranquility, then we have to track in slow and careful to the Apollo site. 'Then let's go, Team First Footprint!' Helmet on (and that does nothing for your hair, as Sidibe never stops telling me) and out of Theon Habitat. Good little humpie. Good little rover. I swear it looks ready and eager. The seats lower. I think my butt can take it. Seats up, safety bars down.

'Jair?'

'Yes, Cari?'

'Take us out.'

Redrover rolls forward, then turns a sharp three-sixty and takes us back along its own wheel-ruts.

'Jair, what are you doing!' I yell. 'Get us back on the right way.'

'I don't think I can, Cari.'

Redrover is picking up speed. Dust plumes high behind us. This is a machine in a hurry.

'Explain, please?'

'It's not me, Cari. I'm shut out of the controls.'

My head feels the size of the moon. My helmet feels the size of my thumb. At the same time. This is possible, when your rover turns rogue on you. Everything is wrong, everything is throbbing, my cheeks are burning, my breathing is loud, and I don't know what to do. Is this shock? Whatever it is, I hear on the common channel that I'm not the only one.

'Dolores knows,' Jair says. 'She found out what I did with her account. She's changed her passwords. I can't get in. She's bringing us back to Meridian.'

We all hear the weird howl on the common channel. If there were wolves on the moon, that howled at the full Earth, they would sound as destroyed and hopeless as that sound. You'd think no human voice could produce a sound like that. It can. I've heard it before, when the Storm hits Kobe.

'Emer.'

Last person I want to talk to is you, Sid, but I click her channel.

'I'll do this,' I say.

'Are you sure? I mean . . .'

I cut her off.

'I'll do this.'

And I open a private channel to Kobe. I choose a little dancing boy icon from Redrover's emoticon library and set him spinning and tumbling on Kobe's HUD. Kobe likes dancing, though he is unable to dance.

'K K K K K,' I say. 'Oh, K K K K?'

Little games and rhymes, rituals only we know, riddles to which he knows the answer (grammar! see?): these are the ways of Kobe Saito.

The wail breaks into stuttering breaths. Redrover races us west, ever west.

'Oh, K K K K K?' I say again.

'E E, E E E. E E E E, E E,' Kobe says.

Codes match. Protocols established. Even if he used the initial to my old name. Sometimes, sacrifices must be made.

'Kobe, I need you to do something for me. Only you can do it.'

A long pause. That's another kilometre gone.

'K E.'

The storm is passing.

'You know when you took control of Redrover, when Jair got hit by the rock.'

'Yes.'

'Can you do that again?'

'I can't do that, Cariad.'

'For the mission?' Another kilometre-long silence. 'For me?'

'I can't do that because there isn't a medical emergency.'

I almost say *fuck*. Kobe doesn't like people swearing, even though Laine is the sweariest person I know, and it's in my DNA too: the Irish are swear-folk. Swearing makes his head squirm, Kobe says.

'But,' Kobe says.

'But?'

'It is possible to initiate a full local-override.'

'You can do that?'

'I can,' Kobe says, and I remember never to ask him rhetorical questions.

'Make it so,' I say, which I heard is a thing captains say.

'Redrover, protocol 919,' Kobe says on the common channel. 'Override Dolores Santa-ana, executive control to Kobe Saito.'

*You have executive control, Kobe Saito,* says Redrover.

'Turn her around!' I shout. Kobe issues a string of code. And Redrover slows, Redrover turns, Redrover heads back along its well-worn track. We cheer Kobe Saito, Department of Overrides. We cheer even louder as we speed past Theon humpie for the second time, come to the end of our tracks, and then go beyond them, out onto the perfect, unmarked regolith, into the world of adventure.

———————

What is it with Kobe? I'll tell you what it is with Kobe. Someone's got to look out for him. This place isn't easy for someone with his gifts. Laine would if she could, but she's in demand and doesn't always have the time. Morven his enabler is great, but you can't be in colloquium twenty-eight days a lune. So it falls to Cariad Corcoran. Me.

I can see how that might sound like it's a duty, or a contract. It's not. Really. Believe. No, I'm not over-saying. What was that expression you used? No, the other one. 'Protests too much.' Huh. I like that.

No, I'm not a ceegee. And I am absolutely not a mother. He needs someone who knows him and knows the world to make sure they get along together. That's all.

Yes, of course I care.

Yes. Yes, if you want to put it like that. I love him.

---

Fanfares! Telenovela music! Big fuck-off chords! That weird bass-y hommmm thing they use when they want to say *portentous*. Let's pump this up, because it's the Third Act: Team First Footprint has entered Apollo-land!

God and his Mother, it's boring. Flat flat flat flat.

'Well, it is the Sea of Tranquility,' Kobe says, which is as close as he comes to a joke. The only highlight is the West Tranquility Moonloop tower, and that soon falls behind our wheels.

'Are we headed right?' Jair asks as dust dust dust rolls under our wheels. Then I see it. Oh, I see it. West of northwest, a pimple on the chin of the moon. I zoom in my HUD, the resolution is terrible, but there is no mistaking the boxy body, the spindly legs.

'Is that real?' Jair asks, and it's a reasonable question because it looks nothing like anything else I've seen on the moon, built or natural.

'That is the descent stage of the Apollo 11 lunar module,' I say. 'That's where they landed and walked. Kobe, take us in.'

'Um,' Sidibe says. I do not like her um. 'Don't you

think maybe we should leave Redrover here and walk? Maybe not run our tyre tracks over everything?'

'Kobe,' I say, but he's already parked Redrover. Seats down, safety bars up; boots on the regolith. Single file so as to create as few stray footprints as possible. Me leading—of course. We walk towards the Apollo.

No ghosts on the moon, everyone says. Cariad Corcoran says different. There are ghosts in Tranquility. Not dead people, spooks, things that throw things. These are ghosts like memories. Old things. History ghosts. This place, these machines, are history. It's a hundred years since Apollo 11, but this place feels ancient. This is the heart of the moon, yet it feels nothing like my moon. Alien and ghosty.

'They're so vile, these Apollo-nauts,' Jair says. The landing site is strewn with abandoned experiments, equipment, throw-away gear. Tools and food pouches. Piss bags. Radiation has worn away the plastic, and the contents have drained or evaporated. Shit sacks. These are more enduring. The site is well documented: I've given everyone the inventory. One hundred and eight objects. That mirror-array thing was used to bounce a laser back to Earth. Distance down to five millimetres. Amazing they could get accuracy like that back then. Amazing they could even get here. I stop at a pair of moonboots, one left lying across the other as if the man who walked in them had been sucked up into heaven. We all get pictures.

'Maybe that's where we get it from,' Sidibe says. We are a filthy folk, us moonkind. The surface is covered with our junk. Old bunkers and habitats, dead rovers. Redundant graders and sinterers. Anything old and outmoded and obsolete. It dies, we dump. Send it up to the surface. Out of sight, out of mind. But what about the zabbaleen, you might ask? They care about the rare. Metal is cheap, metal is everywhere. We can make gold by clicking our fingers. But what use is gold? What's precious is us-stuff. Life-stuff. So we use and throw, smelt and chuck. Messy messy moonfolk. And the dust; always the dust, forever the dust.

'Right, so, careful now,' I say because we are among the footprints. They are big, fat, ridged things, more paws than boots. 'Hey, Jair: neko feet!' He doesn't answer and my joke feels stupid and wrong. This is a powerful place. It requires respect. And now we are in the middle of Tranquility Base. I can reach out and touch the Apollo module's leg. I can read the words on the plaque wrapped around that leg. *Here men from the planet Earth first set foot upon the Moon, July 1969 A.D. We came in peace for all mankind.* Names: *Neil A. Armstrong; Michael Collins; Edwin E. Aldrin, Jr.; Richard Nixon, President, United States of America.* Who is this Richard Nixon? The United States of America. There is its flag, lying there where the launch-blast felled it, bleached white by hard sun and radiation. I try to make out a pattern: stars, bars? Ghosts.

Here, among the bootprints, is the very first one. I try to imagine Neil Armstrong's boot one metre above the regolith, where nothing has ever set foot before, one centimetre and the dust still perfect like it's been for four billion years. And touchdown . . .

I try to imagine the people back in the United States of America, people all around the world watching that foot. I've seen it, of course, it's part of our history education, but here I can see it. I turn my foot in the dust and my sasuit boot's feedback conducts the powdery crunch to my nerve endings.

Was he scared? Neil?

I'm not scared here. But I am awed.

'Where is it?' Kobe asks, and my HUD shows me. It's not clean, it's not clear, there are other ridged prints across most of it, but by my research (and I researched this): here is the First Footprint.

'Here,' I say, and flick the overlay to everyone's HUDs. And then I see it. Alongside the mess of prints that make up humanity's first steps on the moon: the clear, present, and unmistakable tread of a sasuit boot. We're not the first. As I see it, everyone else sees and makes the same realisation.

'Fuck,' Jair says, and I feel my bones and muscles sag as if the Apollo Module somehow brought Earth gravity with it and I am six times heavier and more exhausted.

I don't know what to do. I think my mouth may be open. Then Sidibe kneels down, tells Kobe to hold her left arm, and leans way forwards. She brushes out the alien footprint, careful and delicate as surgery.

'Get the picture,' she says. 'Quick. And we never tell anyone about this.'

I order everyone into position between the footprint and the body of the lunar lander. Sidibe unzips the camera from her wrist, sets it on the regolith, and joins us. Sidibe, Jair, me in the front, arms around each other; big big Kobe behind us, arms around all of us.

'Just getting it in focus,' Sidibe says. 'Smile.'

'You can't see it,' Kobe says.

'You see it,' Sidibe says. 'You feel it. Smile!'

So I smile and shit me but she's right, I feel it spread through me like relief and heat and electricity. I stand straight, I stand strong. I stand like I'm smiling. Because we made it. Team First Footprint found the First Footprint. We did it. We sneaked out of Queen of the South. We rode the maglev. We battled barf and sealed a suitbreach and rerouted Redrover.

(This is how I am going to tell it forever.)

And here we stand. Arms around each other, secret smiles, hand gestures and moves and dabs.

'Happy wedding, Laine and Gebre!' Kobe says. Oh, right. We do it again, do it right, and Sidibe streams it to her camera. Last of all she gets a close-up of the Armstrong footprint.

'I'm going to make a printout,' she says. 'I think we should have an actual thing.' Kobe wants one too, then Jair, and Cariad Corcoran isn't going to be left out so I add my name to the list and it's not such a bad idea, having a *thing*. Things say this object, event, footprint is worth bringing into the solid world.

At last we break the pose. And I feel good. Better than I thought, considering we cleaned up the site for the picture, considering we weren't the first, considering it was just one in a whole mess-up of footprints.

'Right, so, team,' I say. 'We got what we came for. Let's go back.' I say that and the smiles goes out of me, out of all of us. Back there is the shit-rain of weddings and new family and everything changing and trying to talk round the expenses we ran up and having to explain what we did and why (which is harder, because out here on the dust plains of the Tranquility, I'm not so sure myself anymore). Before we go, I make sure to leave my own footprint beside Neil Armstrong's. Cariad Corcoran was here. That's all we can ever really say, in my philosophy.

The universe is big, space is cold, stars are balls of gas and the moon want to kill you, but you can whisper, *I was here.*

That's why.

---

Why shouldn't I have a philosophy? Everyone's got a philosophy. Even you, machine. You've got all that binary, hetero-normative, sex-obsessed, bio-parentist, nuclear-family-oriented Freudian stuff. Did I leave any out?

Neo-Freudian. Right, so: but that's a philosophy, isn't it? That's a belief system. Yes, it is. It affects what you say, how you behave, how you deal with people. With me. Believing is what believing does, otherwise would we know you believe it? Philosophy is action.

So you could say, Cariad Corcoran's philosophy took her to the Sea of Tranquility and the First Footprint.

You think it's bleak? I think it's beautiful. Poetic.

But I'm not going to talk about it anymore because now I need to tell you what Kobe saw.

---

Well, it what's Kobe said, rather than what Kobe saw, because we don't see it until he makes the noise. So it's not even really what Kobe said; it's what Kobe grunts. Except it was more like a *whoa*.

Kobe: *Whoooooa!*

Long, like that. We look where he's looking and see what he's seeing.

A rover—a big one—parked up alongside our Redrover. Five suits standing around Little Red. A cable connecting the two rovers.

'What are they doing?' Kobe says, and before I can tell him to leave it to me, he's off, full pelt. Those shell-suits have power-assist. They run fast.

'Leave it alone!' Sidibe shouts even though whoever they are, they can't hear her on our channel, and before I can give any order, she's off as well and even non-power-assisted she's only a couple of footprints behind Kobe.

Footprints. We're stomping all over humanity's first steps on another world.

Fuck it. In for a cent, in for a bitsie.

'Jair, let's go!'

And we run, not caring where our boots go. Because I have a horrible gut-sick feeling about those people and their cable.

Sidibe is helmet-to-helmet with one of the suits. There are geometric patterns on the helmet and gloves: adinkra, the symbol system of the Asamoahs. I read some adinkra: a sort-of G with like a nail through it: Ohene

Tuo. The King's Gun. These are blackstars and that is their captain. Four stand around the captain, two more guard the cable between their rover and Little Red. Good people don't stand like that.

'What's going on?' I ask on the common channel.

'They're stealing our power!' Sidibe shouts, loud enough to hurt, then launches into a stream of Akan that I am sure is so full of curses even Laine would raise an eyebrow.

'Stop it!' I shout.

A channel opens.

'No,' says the King's Gun. A woman's voice. Moonborn accent.

'Kobe! Save Redrover!' I shout. And Kobe wills his armour forwards and his right arm swings, woosh, and his left arm swings, woosh, and the blackstars fly back because if one of those fists connects with a helmet, it's going to take more than a squirty gun of sealant to make it all vac-tight again. Kobe seizes the cable and wrenches it from Redrover's charging socket.

'Now, that was rash,' the Asamoah woman says, and Sidibe is on her back on the regolith and the King's Gun has a knee on her chest and the tip of a knife at the place where helmet seal meets sasuit. 'Behave.'

My head is full of noise and numb; thick dust and clouds of smoke; ideas, images, words, but I can't touch any of them. I am helpless. The world of stories is full of brilliant martial arts moves and last-ditch escapes and cunning plans where we win. The world of real doesn't allow these things. Anything I do could get us hurt. Killed.

This is adventure. I hate you, adventure.

'Kobe, leave it.'

I hear the wail growing inside him, bubbling.

'Kobe, it's all right.'

It's not all right. It's so not all right.

'Kobe, please.'

The growl fades. He steps back to my side.

'Wise.' The woman speaks in Akan and the blackstars plug the cable back into Redrover. I imagine I can hear the life blood being sucked out: Little Red turning to Little Pink turning to Little Beige. Deadrover.

'Leave us something!' I shout. 'We have to get back.'

'Where's back?' the Ohene Tuo says.

'Meridian,' Jair says.

'That's not going to happen,' the Ohene Tuo says. 'Forget about that.'

'You can't just leave us!' I shout. Sidibe gets to her feet. She's slow and scared and her vital signs are flickering red all over my HUD.

'I can,' the woman says. 'Out here I can do anything. You have to get back to Meridian, I have to get back to Twé.'

'I would have given you some,' I shout back.

'You see, I can't stake my crew's lives on your "give" and your "some",' the Ohene Tuo says. 'You have a mission, I have a mission. There's only enough power for one mission and I have the resources, strength, and numbers to ensure that it is my mission that succeeds.'

'Give us some back,' I say. I am cold, so cold I feel myself shivering. It's not cold-cold—vacuum is the best insulator; the problem up on the surface isn't cold but too much heat. Listen to me, I'm getting like Kobe: taking refuge in facts. This cold is inside my head: among the dust and stuff tumbling there are numbers and they grind and mill and stick to each other, number to number, into equations that are cold and hard and the scariest things I have ever seen.

'Can't take the risk,' the Ohene Tuo says. She speaks in Akan and her blackstars disconnect the socket. It retracts like some sick kind of monster-penis into the belly of their big rover. She raises a hand, turns a finger, and her blackstars jump back into their seats. 'We're powered. And a little over. Left you enough to get you to the big dig at Hypatia, if you're careful. But I wouldn't hang around. Sun-storm coming. You'll want rock over your head when she hits. Take care. Thanks for the power. Moon is hard, baa.'

And they plug up and close up and drive off. On our

power. Our stolen power. Big plumes of dust from their six big wheels. I watch them over the horizon and my brain is bursting and my cheeks are burning and my heart is a mess of molten steel. I have never been so angry. I have never been so humiliated. I have never been so helpless.

'What are we waiting for?' Jair swings himself up into his seat. 'You heard what she said. There's a storm coming.'

The last thing I want is to be on that rover. I can't even bear the thought of the feel of the seat under me. To even touch it is to take in the pollution, the ruin of all the greatness we felt only a few minutes ago. All gone. All puffed away like air from a broken helmet. I feel stupid, I feel like moon and Earth and yes, fuck it, sun are all looking at me and shaking their heads.

'Cari.' I wince at the sound. Cariad. See? She even gives herself a stupid name. 'We need to move. We got beaten and beaten bad, and that hurts, but that's not important. What's important is what we do now.'

'Yes,' I say. Jair's is the only voice that cuts through the high-pitched whine in my head, the noise you get when you want to cry, need to cry, but you cannot must not will not. 'Yes. I have to fix this. Kobe?'

He's already in his seat.

'Lay in a course for Hypatia.'

117

'Yes, Cari.'

And I can bear my name. When Kobe says it, it sounds like respect. We're in the place beyond shit, the tank where the zabbaleen store all the shit and piss of an entire city, up to our noses: robbed blind, maybe enough power to get to safety before the solar storm hits and floods Nearside with charged particles, but who do they turn to? Cariad Corcoran.

'Sidibe.' No answer. No movement. This is bad bad bad. 'Sidibe, come on.' I take her arm and guide her to her seat, settle her in, pull down the safety bars. Nothing. 'Kobe, take us out.' I hardly notice the thrum of the engines, the surge of acceleration as we cut a wide arc in the regolith and drive west-southwest. I'm trying to reach Sidibe. I open a private channel. She flicks me away. I lean my head against the crash bars, trying to get close enough to feel the vibrations of whatever is going on inside her own helmet. The Asamoah woman pulled a knife on her. Had her on her back. Blade at her throat. Didn't matter that she was a kid. She was coming between the King's Gun and the thing she needed to save her crew.

I think Sidibe may be crying, all alone in her helmet.

I'm glad I can't hear her. It might get me crying too, and if I started, I'm afraid that I might not be able to stop.

———

Eight kays short of Hypatia, Redrover runs out of power. It's no surprise: Little Red had been warning us every kay for the last fifteen. I told Kobe to shut it off. What's the point in being warned of something you can't avoid?

We roll to the gentle halt on the edge of the small crater in the southwesterly corner of the Sea of Tranquility. Kobe has to find the manual release to drop us all to the rego.

'People,' Jair says, 'we killed Redrover.'

'You all right?' I say to Kobe on a private channel. I can hear the catch in his breathing but I haven't time for Kobe-wrangling. Or Sidibe-wrangling or anyone-wrangling. We need to move. I've run the numbers. Cold cold numbers. Eight kays, normal walking pace, allowing for fumble time getting into an unfamiliar lock: we will arrive at Hypatia on the last breath of suit power. No power, your suit dies and pretty soon after you die. I'd thought, well, maybe I could run some of the power from Redrover's cells into the suit cells. My conclusion: Redrover was faster and surer than four kids in suits; so burn its batteries to the ground. Now it's strictly by numbers, and even a few minutes' delay is the difference between stepping smiling into a living breathing habitat and falling in as zabbaleen fodder.

'I'm sad,' Kobe says. 'But we have to move on, don't we?'

'We do, Kobe.'

I give the rules. We have to conserve every milliwatt of power. So: essentials only. No comms apart from me, no HUDs apart from Jair, who, as Sidibe still isn't acknowledging an external universe, is now Department of Surface Activities. Peril fucking Suits. The big decision is who gets to navigate. Navigation HUDs don't draw much power, but it's some power. Problem for Cariad Corcoran: Kobe has no sense of direction, Jair is monitoring everyone else, I'm on comms, and Sidibe is orbiting Planet Trauma. So—swallow hard, be the Adult in the Room—the solution to Cariad Corcoran's problem is: Cariad Corcoran.

Jair and Kobe line up behind me.

'Sidibe?'

Not a word, but she falls in behind Big Kobe. Kobe pats Redrover's wheel as we set off up the low crater rim. Kobe is my big worry. Shell-suits store more power, but they eat more power too. I think I have the numbers right. I need to have the numbers right. Then there is Jair: is he reading the signs right, will he know if anything goes wrong and if it does will he tell me? And Sidibe, who is like walking death . . . Everyone is my big worry. Especially me.

———

It goes like this. Walk walk walk walk walk. Rocks, stones, crater big, crater small, crater just right. Stones, rocks. In the distance, west of us, the pickup platform of the South West Tranquillitatis Moonloop tower. The main body of the tower—two kilometres tall—is down under the horizon. Up there in the golden west the big golden sun is getting ready to spew out all manner of cosmic shit over her planetary family, their moons, and Team First Footprint. Stones, rocks. Sound effects: suit systems clicking, cooler creaking, rustle of dust through the boot soles, and the only other three people in the world (it seems) breathing hard and heavy in your ear.

Then there's a hiss on my comms. A private channel opening.

'Emer?'

I let it go. I also let it go that I and only I command the comms.

'Hey.'

'E . . . Cariad.'

My name. She called me by my name.

'Are you all right?'

I know. It's dumb and it's a cliché and it means absolutely nothing (right? What does that mean? And all right?), but you have to unlock the door before someone can push it open. I hear her breathe deep.

'I'm so angry,' she says. 'Just so angry. I can't even begin—'

She breaks off. She hears the catch in my breath. That catch of breath? Because I'm scared scared scared that she blames me for what happened to her. I brought her to Tranquility, I talked her into coming in the Prince Igor banya in Queen; I had the idea of an expedition to the First Footprint because I couldn't deal with my mum marrying her dad; because I hated the idea of having a new derecha who was shinier, smarter, braver, better than me. That everyone knows this. Kobe, Jair. That everyone has always known this. That everyone blames me for everything. That I am the sick heart of all evil.

All this in one catch of the breath. Breath comes before talk.

'It's not you,' Sidibe says. She knows me too well. Her voice hardens. 'Why should it be you? Why does it always have to be Cariad Corcoran? This is nothing to do with you. That woman attacked me. Put me on the ground. I hate saying that. It makes my skin feel like fingers all over it. It makes me feel polluted.'

I almost say *Sorry*, then pull the word back. Sorry would make it about me again. She's right. This is nothing to do with me. This is all Sidibe's. I can't feel what she felt, on the ground, under the hand of a bigger and stronger woman. I can't feel her helplessness. I can't feel all her self-belief, all those times that Gebre told her she was great and golden and special, all that confidence and pride, torn from her in a second like someone ripped her wings from her shoulders. I can imagine, I can conjure up a feeling, but it's not what she felt, on her back, under the knife. All I can do is listen.

I listen.

Sidibe has much to say.

At the end of it, I begin to understand Sidibe Sisay.

---

As Sidibe talks, as she spills and flows and I listen, I am also watching the power indicator in the corner of my visor drop from yellow through orange and red to pink towards the white.

Kobe breaks radio-hygiene. *Look!* Look at what, Kobe? Grey, greyer, grey-most? Oh, right, so: he's that much taller in that shell-suit than the rest of us and he's seen a thing we can't. Yet. One minute on, I see the tips of Hypatia's comms towers over the horizon and I am so filled with joy I feel nauseous. Sick-happy. I didn't know that could be a thing.

I make it to the main lock on the very edge of white. Seven minutes of power left. We tumble into the lock chamber, plug into the charge points, and watch the door close. Someone has spray-painted a Lady Luna on the inside of the outlock door, one part of her face on each half. Black life and white death coming together. Lady Luna: you got emotions I can't even begin to explain. Numb-afraid. Happy-vom. Now dread-relief. Relief that we made it to Hypatia. Dread that something else is waiting beyond the inlock door.

'Um, folk,' Jair says. That *Um* again. 'The lock? It's not pressurising.'

'Is there something wrong with the lock mechanism?' I ask.

'No,' Jair says. 'There's something wrong with Hypatia.'

The lock cycle completes, the inlock door plots. HYP left, ATIA right. Ahead is an elevator platform. We ride it down—what else can we do?—into relief-dread. Now the suits are recharged, the HUDs on all our visors are telling us the same thing: *This is your sixty-minute air warning. Sixty minutes.*

Hard light blinds us; when the visors have darkened, we see the reason.

Hypatia is a bustling, thriving city of seven thousand residents located in southwest Mare Tranquillitatis. Hypatia is an important research and industrial centre and a major interchange between Equatorial One and the branch lines to Sinus Asperitatis and Mare Nectaris. Or Hypatia will be when Hypatia is finished. Right now, Hypatia is a construction site.

The elevator dumps us onto the middle deck of a massive scaffold rig in what will be Hypatia's main station, which is just a big big tube carved from raw rock, two kilometres long, straight as truth. That blinding light is from dozens of work-arrays; even in the hot glare I can't see all the way to the end of the tunnel. Dust. Always. Dust. There is an atmosphere in Hypatia. It's made of dust. Machines. I can feel the rattle and rumble and shakey-shake through the metalwork. Maybe a good thing there is no air in here: it would be like being inside the Blessed Angel Michael's own trumpet.

Amalia, three derecho-wards around the ring, plays trumpet. Jazz trumpet. I've heard her. I don't understand her music—too many notes—but I did ask her why she didn't blow out her cheeks like a festival balloon, like I've seen in the archives. That's bad technique, she says. Bad technique.

'Is there anyone here?' I ask. I said about being inside a trumpet. There's another thing I saw in the archives of Earth: insects. Crass things called termites, all white and pasty, that live in tunnels inside these huge mounds in the hot places on Earth, which is kind of everywhere now. They scurry about in those tunnels, millions of them, up and down, across the roof, all over. They scared me until I realised that they were really, really small, then they scared me because there were millions of them. A million tinies is worse than one big, don't you think?

The machines in this tunnel are like termites, up and down, across the roof, all over.

And this is just one tunnel of an entire city.

I see patterns shift on Jair's HUD; he's into the city's network, squeezing into places that only a smart neko can go.

'Um, Cari.'

I'm not going to like this.

'We're the only living things here. Everyone else moved out. The solar storm.'

'We're underground, aren't we?' I say, and I can't believe why I'm arguing. 'Big rock up there.'

'Maybe they thought, because it's not sealed yet, better safe?' Jair says.

'We are safe, aren't we?' Kobe says.

Before I can say, *We are, trust me, Kobe,* my suit pings. *Cariad, fifty minutes of air remaining. Fifty minutes.* Since recharging in the elevator, I have all my HUDs and monitors back. I must have been breathing deep and anxious because in the next few minutes I have to captain like I have never captained before.

'Jair, can you find us air?'

He knows what I just heard.

'There's an airplant about a kay down the tunnel up on

the top level,' Jair says and highlights it on my map over-lay. It's high.

'Wait,' I say, but Kobe and Jair are already loping down the gantry. Sidibe is right at Jair's shoulder. It's not right that that bothers me. I know. But it does.

The airplant is a chunk of industrial tech half the size of Redrover. It's big and it's high. It's very high. A thirty-metre climb. Sidibe is halfway up before I can blink. Kobe is behind her like one of those killer bots you see in nightmares, coming for you hand-over-hand, hand-over-hand. Even Jair has hooked claws over bars. He calls down to me.

'You coming, Cari?'

'Right . . . so.'

I look up. Sidibe is already at the top, swinging out one-handed to look down at me. I can't look at her, I can't look at Kobe and Jair. My head turns inside my head. I know that makes no sense. Since when does how we feel make sense? I see myself up there, climb-ing up the struts, and my head turns inside my head and I fall backwards.

'Cari?'

I'm already falling, falling in my head, falling forever.

'I can't.' Those words: the hardest I have ever said. The ones that follow are the easiest. They just fall from my lips. 'I can't climb, right? I can't go up there.' This is

the bridge in Meridian again, except that was just walking, this is climbing, holding, trusting my hands and
feet. 'I'm scared of heights!'

It's said. It's out. And no one questions it, no one says
anything about how come the big leader can't have
heights, no one says anything about *me*. Jair drops to my
side. He makes little cat-paw to me. Three jumps and
Sidibe is at my other side. She rests her hand in the small
of my back, just under my suitpack.

We're down on the catwalk and the air is up there. The
air, and Kobe, clinging to the rigging like an all-avenging
battle-mecha.

'I think I can get this!'

'Kobe, it's too heavy!' I shout.

'I got powers in this suit,' Kobe says and pulls himself
onto the upper walkway. He pushes the airplant towards
the edge. He makes it look easy. He has true powers in
that suit. Now is the tricky bit; he has to get the airplant
off the walkway with one hand and lower himself down
the rig with the other. He crouches, creeps. Keep the
centre of gravity low. He reaches for a handhold, misses.
Wobbles. I see it happen. We all see it happen and none
of us can do a thing about it. The centre of gravity shifts,
the airplant tumbles. Falls. Kobe falls with it. His fingers
are locked to the frame.

I shout. We all shout. The common channel is cries

and yells. The airplant hits our catwalk, tumbles forwards. Kobe whiplashes through the air. He arcs, he flies, he hits the ground far, far below. He is very small, he is very far away.

'Fuck,' Jair says.

His monitor: I can't even begin to take in all the things that are broken. The big one, the immediate one, is that his suit is cracked. That's serious, but the suit can deal with it the same way it dealt with the vom: seal him from the neck up. Human skin is pretty pressure-tight—sasuits are designed to work with that. The big one, the one that will kill him, is his helmet. He's leaking air through a dozen cracks. The bars on my monitor are pink edging white. My suit HUD offers to show me a minute countdown. No fucking thank you, suit.

'Kobe,' I say on the common channel, then on every channel. 'Kobe . . . Talk to me.'

I don't know what to do. I don't know what to *do*.

Sidibe leaps from the catwalk. She drops down the face of scaffold, straight down. She can't land like that; even in our gravity she'll shatter both ankles. She flexes, some incredible, limber flyer thing, and launches herself off the trusses. Her timing is incredible. Impossible. She flies out, away from the steel, somersaults, reorients herself to hit the ground safely. Lands braced, sprung, poised a spit and hop from Kobe.

'Fuck,' Jair says again.

Before you learn to fly, you learn to fall.

She snaps open a pocket on her utility belt. I make out a tube of sealant spray in her dust-smudged golden glove.

'Sidibe, I love you!' I shriek.

'First rule of moonwalking,' Sidibe says. She works the spray over Kobe's visor. 'Sealant first, sealant last, sealant always.'

'Where did you get it?' I ask.

'Took it from Redrover when we left it,' Sidibe says. 'One at each seat, remember?' She lifts Kobe's head to run the spray around the back of his helmet. Every first aid guide says don't do that, never do that, never move a potential spine injury. Neck and spine they can fix. Death by anoxia is more problematic. 'How's his pressure?'

The bars are rising out of red to green. His reserve: that's scary. And Kobe's not moving, not speaking.

'Jair, can you check if there's anything working on that airplant?'

He's more careful than Sidibe, but I still can't watch him go down the grid, paw over paw. He works around the airplant. Even I can see that one corner is smashed in.

'Not good, Cari.'

Kobe still isn't moving. His pressure may be good, but he's lost a lot of breathables. A lot. I make a decision.

'Sidibe, is it possible to run air from one suit to another?'

'It's a standard feature,' Sidibe says.

'Right, so: Sidibe, Jair, I want you to give him some of your air.' I am aware, oh very aware, that they are down there with Kobe and I am up on the catwalk where I can't run a line to his suit. That I am asking something I can't do myself. 'I'll tell you when it's enough.'

'Right,' Sidibe says. Without an order from me, she finds the airline in Kobe's suit and hooks it to her suit-pack. I watch the bars rise, the bars drop.

'Right, so: that's enough. Jair?'

He hesitates.

'Jair, Kobe needs you.'

'What about you, Cari?'

'I'll donate some when he gets back up here.'

'If he gets back up there,' Jair says. For a moment I think he might break the team and show himself to be so not the Jair I always knew and loved. As an iz: you need to know that. As an iz. And that is more heart-breaking even than the thought of us dying here together and the construction workers coming back after the sun-storm and finding our huddled bodies—not because that can't happen—it can happen too too easily; happens to people every day when they get careless or clever or show-offy—but because there is something romantic in it all ending like that and everyone being sorry that we were dead but we were together, friends to the end, and there is nothing romantic about someone you've grown up with, you've shared ceegee and home and colloquium with, being so mean they'd cling onto a few puffs of air for a few minutes more breathing.

Not so cute, neko.

'Kobe will be back up there,' I say from my high place, and Jair slides in to unhook the line from Sidibe's suit-pack and into his own. I monitor the levels with care and complete justice. Not a breath more than Sidibe gave, not a breath less.

Long time. Long long long time. At last Kobe moves. Arm twitches, head lifts. Sidibe helps him sit up.

'How do you feel, Kobe?' I ask on the common channel.

'I hurt,' he says.

'Can you climb, Kobe?' I ask.

He hauls himself upright. It is like rocks coming to life. Even from the catwalk I can see what his answer will be. And it is.

*Thirty minutes,* the suit monitor tells me.

'Jair, you get up there,' Sidibe says. 'Kobe, can I like, ride on your back?'

Shell-suits shrug pretty good. Sidibe slides around behind Kobe, wraps legs around his waist, one arm around his neck. The other arm, I can't see what it's doing but it's busy busy. Jair flips onto the catwalk beside me. And Kobe staggers to his feet, takes one step two step three step four, big gallumphing mecha steps. Sidibe clings to his back.

'Like Kobe said, there's always an override,' she says.

'How are you doing that?' I ask.

'I jacked into his suit comms line,' Sidibe says.

Kobe climbs the rig now, one hand reaching slowly up, grasping firm and sure, one heavy boot lifting, finding safe footing. Slow and relentless as death, Sidibe like a tiny bright child in a kiddie-sling.

This is not a thing I will unsee any time soon.

Kobe clambers up onto the catwalk. Sidibe moves to sit on his shoulders, legs around his neck.

'You still driving him?' I ask on her private channel.

'I need to,' Sidibe says.

I make sure Jair sees me run air into Kobe's suit.

*Twenty-four minutes' air remaining.*

Captain Cariad got to captain.

'We need to get out of here. Jair, did the construction folk leave any transport at all?'

More neko-magic.

'There's a Taiyang 224 in the west lock,' Jair says. 'It's about a kay and a half and all the way up.'

'Could it get us to Twé?'

The name still makes me burn with humiliation, but fuck it; it's the closest major city. I will find you, King's Gun, some year, and Cariad Corcoran will remind you of what you took, and we will have a settling of accounts.

'It's got four hours' air, so it could, Cari.' Everyone hears the unspoken *but*.

Someone has to say it. Might as well be Captain Cariad.

'The but?'

'Twé's a hundred and seventy-five kays west. Kobe?'

'The top speed of the Taiyang 224 is one hundred and twenty kph,' my Department of Transport says. His serious, dull voice is like dance music to me. 'If we run it at full speed, our best time to Twé is an hour twenty or so. That's with full battery charge. If I knew the charge level, I could calculate it against air reserves more precisely . . .'

'It doesn't matter!' Jair cuts across Kobe on the common channel. 'Full or empty, it doesn't fucking matter! There's a storm coming? Remember? A full-on fucking solar storm hits the moon in forty-four minutes. This is not if, perhaps, maybe. This is sure as fucking death. If we are out when it hits, we burn. And here's our options. We go up there, we're nuked. We stay down here, we suffocate. Time to get fucking serious. We need to stop playing games. We need to stop being stupid. We need to call for help. We need to get on the comms array and tell someone to fucking rescue us. The adventure is over.'

'Um,' Kobe says, and him using Jair's um is the worst thing. That um is the glass spike through the heart. Because what Cariad Corcoran does is run the numbers, run the numbers, run the numbers, and before Kobe gets to um, she knows that help won't reach us in time. From Twé? The numbers run both ways. We can't get to them so they can't get to us. From Meridian? Forget it. VTO is building a fleet of rescue ships: when it's complete they will be able to reach anywhere on the moon in fifteen minutes. Right now, they've got three. Even if the nearest one launches now, it'll be making final descent and landing through a slew of solar protons. (I researched this too. Got to do something on your long lonely moonwalk.)

I tell them this. I tell them what the numbers say, and what they say is that rescue will not come out of the sky on burning blue fire. After I tell them this they are very solemn and quiet.

I turn off the monitors. They're just showing what your body will tell you all too soon soon soon.

Ideas: where do they come from? I don't know, I think they must always have been there, in bits and pieces, and then something shakes your world and the bits and pieces fall together. And stick. And bob to the surface. I see it. An idea. No, a plan. All there, all at once, and it's brilliant. I can get us out of this. I can get us home all safe and breathing and in time for the wedding. How perfect is that?

'Jair! Call Dolores. Tell her exactly where we are, what's happened.'

'Why me?' Jair protests.

Because you said that. Because I knew you would say that. Because the kitty isn't so cute anymore. But I say, 'Because I need her to use her account for something. Right, so? Kobe: can you get that Taiyang rover going?'

Kobe nods. He almost throws Sidibe. Her arms tighten around his helmet.

'Sidibe, you hold on tight,' I say. 'Because we need to get to that rover superfast.' I take a deep breath. 'Run!'

---

One thing, Kobe: between all the specs and storage and battery life and air supply, you forgot to tell us an important detail about the Taiyang 224.

It's a two-person model.

Which means me and Jair in the seats, Kobe latched onto the rear, and Sidibe riding the LSU and comms on the roof. Bouncing and bounding and leaping over every stone and crater. This rover doesn't have a name—not enough time for that—but it's really hammering it. Flat out. Batteries at burn-out, motors red hot. The clock is ticking. The death clock.

Actually, I don't understand that. Ticking? Making a tick tick tick noise? Why? What's that? Clocks are silent. Even the death clock. Especially, I think, the death clock.

We hit a ridge flat out and all four wheels leave the regolith. In mid-leap, I private-channel Jair.

'Is she pissed off?'

'You know that beyond-pissed-off?'

Too too well, neko.

'Beyond that beyond.'

'Has she done it?'

'Of course she's done it.'

We land hard to a creak and crack of suspension and Sidibe yelping from the roof.

'Can you take it a little easier?'

No, we cannot. Use your superskills, fly-girl.

It's been on the map HUD forever, the sensors for the past five minutes; now I see the launch platform over the rim of Soleares crater: the South West Tranquillitatis Moonloop tower.

I'm taking us home the long way, right around Mother-moon.

------

The Mackenzies mine the metal, the Asamoahs farm; the Suns run the IT, the Vorontsovs move the moon. So, that's a slight overstatement, but VTO operates everything that moves or crawls or flies Nearside and Farside, from the old rover-bus lines to the maglevs to those sexy new moonships that won't be coming to rescue us, but most of all, they run the Moonloop, and without it nothing on the moon makes any sense. Those Mackenzie rare earths: how do they ship them back to Earth? The Moonloop. Those Jo Moonbeams taking waaaay too big steps and flying through the air with their hands and legs milling, how do they get here, how do they get back, if they decide to go back? The Moonloop. Those university researchers out there on Farside listening to the universe, throwing probes out to all those other worlds: even they need the Moonloop to get there. That new outfit; those Brasilians who have this super-sexy business shipping fuel to Earth's fusion plants: those helium-3 containers all get there via Moonloop.

The Vorontsovs built and maintain the Moonloop. It's a two-hundred-kilometre-long spinning cable of superstrong construction carbon that wheels around the moon in a fast low orbit in one hundred and eighteen minutes. It's like a slingshot. Pick something up from the surface then sling it off to another world: Earth or somewhere more exciting. A momentum transfer tether. I don't understand the fine details, like using a moving mass to change the centre of gravity to compensate for lunar mascons, or to drop down to snatch a cargo pod from a Moonloop tower. All I know, it's up there, and it's rolling towards us.

One hundred and eighteen minutes? You say? You don't have one hundred and eighteen minutes, Cariad Corcoran.

All true. Except, because of the new Corta helium traffic, three lunes ago VTO launched a second tether, and twenty days ago, a third tether.

A tether comes wheeling up over the horizon in fifteen minutes. All we need is to be waiting on the platform.

---

Not literally standing on the platform. That would be buck-madness, as Laine would say. We leave the rover at the hatch. The cargo bay is unpressurised, a big shed with just enough sheeting to keep dust out of the machinery. Footprints, abandoned construction worker kack, porny graffiti on the girders: a lot of Hypatia has come in this way.

'We're getting into that?' Jair asks. I admit, it's a creepy prospect. The cargo pods are cylinders, shackle gear at the top, magnetic clasps at the bottom. A crane's going to lift us, move us to the elevator, and send us two kilometres to the launch platform. It's going to be cosy, four

of us in one of those things. Cosy: that's a slight under-
statement. Claustrophobic. That. And Kobe in that hulk-
ing great shell-suit. And all our twitches and phobias.

No time. We got to do this.

'Kobe, you first,' I say, and in he climbs, ducking
through the low hatch. Even pressed against the wall of
the cylinder, he takes up most of the space. 'Jair.'

'There's no—'

'I don't have time!' I shout.

'It helps to opaque your visor,' Sidibe says. 'Like on
the maglev.' I remember the story she told on Redrover.
Now I understand what was scary: not the rover port that
could have blown at any time; the truly scary was the cosmic ray that went through glass, her bio-mom, her. That
white flash that killed Geetanjali, that could be waiting
for years in her DNA to turn rogue and eat from the inside. Ikh. 'You too, Kobe.' Neko-kitties are slender and
lithe: Jair seems to take up no space at all.

'Sidibe, in,' I say. I'm last. The captain should always
be last. Last out of the airless habitat, last off the rover,
last into the space-lifeboat. 'Jair, close the door.' My suit-
lights let me see how tight-packed I am with my team. I
can feel Sidibe and Jair breathing. Visor to visor to visor.
Poor Kobe is hunched over, his visor almost touching the
top of my helmet. Maybe it would be better to turn vision
off. No. The captain has to be there, whatever.

'Start her up, Jair,' I order.

'Machines got it now,' Jair says. I almost reply, *What if something goes wrong?* I catch myself. What's the point? This either works or it doesn't, and the doesn't can't be thought about. So much that can't be thought about. This can, that spinning cable, the sun-spew billowing towards us, what waits for us when we step out of the capsule in Meridian, the cost, the trouble, the questions, the explanation, the fact that two minutes after Jair told Dolores half the moon, Nearside and Farside, was following our escape, frantic for any news, any rumours.

I order everyone to shut off their social networks. That sort of thing is not good to hear. I lurch against Jair, rebound into Sidibe: the crane has us. We're swinging, a slow, soft pendulum. This can't be stopped now. Another jolt, clicks and clanks I feel through my boots. Upward travel. We're in the elevator.

Time to storm-front eight minutes.

How long does it take to go up two kilometres? I try to imagine the Moonloop wheeling over the highlands east of Sinus Medii, covering in seconds all those dusty, jolting kilometres that took us so long in Redrover. Lovely old Redrover. We betrayed you. We ran you into the dust and abandoned you.

It's a fucking rover, Cariad. A machine. AI or no AI. And I wish I hadn't thought that. Because AIs are almost people. They talk. They think. I'm pretty sure they can feel, be hurt. And thinking this, I also think, this is me, thinking of anything but what is happening to me right now: locked in a metal can, waiting to be flicked off the top of a high tower and slung around the moon, a Hail Mary ahead of a massive solar storm.

I feel machinery moving above my head, the cable shackles opening. The elevator locks unseal. We are here, canned-up and waiting.

'Cari,' Sidibe says. 'We all told you our scary stories. You never told us yours.'

'No,' I say. 'I didn't, did I?'

Acceleration like nothing I have ever felt before grabs me and tries to push me into the floor. A million tons on my head, my legs, a million tons on every organ. I see red, my head swims.

'Fuck,' I whisper and every letter takes a million years. And I go in an instant from multiple-gee to zero-gee. The tether has swung up to the top of its rotation and let go. We are flying free across the Sea of Tranquility. My stomach hits my throat. Do not vom. Whatever happens, whatever you feel, do not vom in free-fall. The next tether in cycle is spinning towards us across the wild highland east of Fecunditatis. It will catch us, spin us up, sling us onwards.

What if it misses?

It's never missed. Like Jair said, machines got it now.

But what if machine ain't got it?

It'll be quick. We'll make our own crater. They might even name it after me. Cariad Crater or Corcoran Crater?

If something did go wrong, I'd know because I have the cold numbers.

Would I tell them they were falling to their deaths?

I like to think I wouldn't.

And then there is another snap and I have weight and momentum and *pain* as the waiting tether locks with the capsule latches and we are swung up and around, too scared to scream, to even sob, and slung out over the craters and tiny lost seas of Farside.

This is the trick of it. This is how we live. We put the body of Lady Luna between us and the sun-squall. She knows a thousand ways to kill you, but sometimes, she saves. But there's always a price. Her price: her shield isn't total. For the last five minutes as the last tether drops us down to Meridian port, we're in the full glare of the sun. Under the nuclear hammer. No way around it. Five minutes shouldn't kill us. Might not even make us sick.

Cariad Corcoran hates hates hates having only bad choices.

I told them that one. I had to. In case like, our hair falls out or something.

Again—*again*—a million tons of shit drops on me. The third tether. A whole thundering turn—my eyes, my brain, are drained of blood and thought, of anything except *get me home, get me home, get me back to Osman Tower*. And free. Streaking out over the Grimaldi and the highlands of east Farside, over west Procellarum, over Maestlin and Lansberg and St Olga: flying home. I'm blind and deaf in this capsule and dumb with fright, but the eye in my mind sees ahead of me the terminator; the line of light and fire where we pass from Lady Luna's shadow into the burning light. One final test. One final catch. The final tether is the first tether, wheeled all the widdershins way around the moon.

This time I scream. This time I open my mouth and my lungs and roar all the way around and all the way down, through the radiation ticking from my suit's comms, the white flashes of charged particles stabbing through my brain. Then the rotation speed of the tether matches the orbital velocity of the moon, we come to rest relative to each other. The latches decouple and we are deposited soft as a kiss on the platform.

I stop screaming and realise my suit comms has been pinging me for over a minute. We're back in the networked world. People need to talk to me.

*1128, 1128?*

I don't recognise the voice. That's a good thing. I don't

recognise the number, wait: yes: that's us. Our capsule ident.

'Hi, this is 1128, Cari—Emer—Corcoran.'

'Hello, 1128, this is Meridian Moonloop Control. What's your status, Emer?'

I blink up the monitors. God and her mother, I will be so so so happy to get out of this helmet. Greens all the way up and all the way down. I think this is what she means when she asks me about *status*.

'We are good,' I say, and then the words open like flowers and I start to laugh. Laugh and laugh and laugh without end. Moonloop Control tries to get a sensible answer out of me but she never will, so in the end she just says, *Bringing you home, 1128,* and I'm sure I hear my laugh in the edges of her voice as we ride the elevator down into the welcoming underground.

We made it. I took us to the First Footprint and escaped energy-bandits and the lost city of Hypatia and flew us right round the whole of the moon and got us all back home again.

Captain Cariad.

'Look,' Sidibe says on the common channel, but all I can see is visors in the gloaming. Then she flicks an image onto my visor, onto all our visors. It's from the Moonloop tower cameras. Earth, half in light, half in night, up at the top of the sky like she always is, ever spinning, never moving. It's winter in the bottom half of the world, and in the dark around the southern pole is a wonder: a scarf of green fire, gleaming, shifting, streaming like a festival dragon. It is beautiful and eerie and makes my heart hurt with all the things I want but can never have. The aurora.

I flick it off my visor.

They should never show you the Earth. This is all we have and it's bare and hard and ugly and wants to kill you, but it's enough. More than enough.

Clamps unlock, I feel us lifted, then set. Moonloop 1128 is docked. The First Footprint Expedition is home.

The capsule door opens. Light spills in. There are people out there. I unlock my helmet and lift it. The adventure is over. Thank fuck.

---

Remember I told you about going out to Nobile to pick up Sidibe's wings from the BALTRAN, and laughing at all the grey, sicky people coming out of the cans?

We looked a lot worse than that, coming off the Moonloop.

---

The medics keep us in for observation in Meridian to

make sure we haven't got anything too fried on our final descent. (Delicate things like Jair and Kobe's balls: me, I got enough—maybe too much?—fat to protect my Fem-parts.) Laine and Gebre have to postpone the wedding. That's another not-happy to add to the Pile of Pissed-nesses. Which is now probably visible from Earth. Not a long postpone, a day or so, but as all the guests have booked travel they're stuck in Queen for three days, and rings have a lot of guests. Oh, you can't imagine how many guests.

Lots of guests is good. Lots of guests can shelter you from a shit-fountain.

And so it's wedding day and we all go to the banya and the beautician and the hair-stylist and print out glorious gear and troop to the park. Gebre's derecha presents the to-be-weds, the commitments are made, the contracts are signed, and the ring is made whole under the tall tall trees. I see Laine facing Gebre and she looks—I cannot lie—fantastic and I feel like a skid-mark in my best pants for fucking up her day. Her day. Not mine. Then they are married and I cheer and clap and set free boxes of party-butterflies and as we all parade to the feast Kobe slides in beside me (he smartens up really good—handsome boy) and whispers, *When do you think we should give her the pictures?*

And I whisper back, *Kobe, never. Ever.*

And you know the worst? On Laine and Gebre's Great Day, all anyone wants to do is ask us about the Expedition. Because we came out of Meridian med-centre famous. Celebrid-ees. Our Adventure became everyone's adventure the moment Jair called home and said, *We need help.* Everyone cared for us, everyone was scared for us, everyone owned us, everyone feels part of our Adventure.

Then the guests go home, the zabbaleen take away the waste, and the wedding clothes go into the reprinter, and there is no shelter from the shit-shower.

It's bad. Not as bad as I feared, because Laine and Gebre are so glad to have us back, to have us whole and alive, to have each other. I've been dreading the expense most. We could have saddled everyone with lifetimes of debt. It's strangely all right. The celebrity helps—Gebre fields nonstop offers from gossip sites until he realised there's money to be made from the gossip sites. He auctions exclusive rights to the story. While we're hot. Celebrity has the shortest half-life of any human-made substance. We go to *LunaLuna!*, the big new gossip network. We're interviewed and profiled individually and together. I sit with Kobe. Jair gets hundreds of you-so-adorables from girls and boys and kids from Meridian to Coriolis, Queen of the South to Rozhdestvenskiy. Sidibe is the breakout star. Of course. In a separate deal she gets offered her own network slot. She turns it down. I think that noble of her. There's talk of a telenovela. I want to know who's in it, but like most of these sort of things, it doesn't go anywhere.

The money is good. Better than good. And when VTO decides that the whole thing is really good publicity for them and their transport system, they write off about forty years of the debt and by the time all the media payments come in, we're in money.

Ten days later, we're cold as yesterday's shit. That's when the consequences arrive. There have to be consequences. We can't get away with our crime and then profit from it. Profit big.

I'm sentenced to house arrest. Hey ho. I can live with that. That's what the network's for. And I've got words and stories and I need to work out a way to make our Adventure into something big and exciting that people will want to buy into. Captain Cariad's Crisis Camp. Peril Suits: Ten Surprising Things You Didn't Know.

To Kobe the time-out from the world is almost philosophical: his universe is already limited and controlled by his own choice: it's how he deals with it.

Sidibe is grounded: literally. Gebre takes her wings away. Three lunes in the no-fly zone. That is cruel and unusual. She goes up to the platform where she took her first flight with us—Osman Tower has put on another ten stories since then, at least—sits with her feet over the edge watching her flyer-friends throwing loops around the towers. I could never do that. Not just the heights; the torture of watching other people doing something I can't.

Thinking about it, that may be how I got us into this in the first place.

Jair: oh, Jair. Dolores sends him to her iz Esteban out at the new Very Large Array build at Tereshkova. Someone comes from Farside, one goes to Farside. Within two days he's turned every head. And loves it. And Esteban is pretty good as a ceegee. Jair's moved across to him and her iz, Chinelo. And, he's realised, the university is a good place for a neko like Jair.

Right, so.

Well, Cariad Corcoran has realised a thing too. It's this, neko. That when you were here, in my home on your ledge and in your perches, when you spent hours perking up your hair into ears and printing out paw-and-claw gloves and obsessing over your makeup; all that time I thought I might have had something with you. You know? Yes, that sort of thing. But I couldn't do anything, because that's the way in rings: anyone but your iz or derecha. But now you're all the way around the moon, in a new link of the ring with new ceegees, so I can, and you know what? I realise I don't want that sort of thing with you. Not just now, I never really did. It was the forbidden fruit thing. (Who forbids fruit? Fruit is good for you. Vitamins and fibre.) Because maybe all those university girls and boys and kids think you're wonderful, but Cariad Corcoran sees through you.

You can be a real shit, Jair.

And, last of all, we get sent for therapy.

———

Which is how I come to be talking to you, machine.

Yes, I know that's machine-ist. Yes, I know I can afford a human counsellor. You think I'm going to spend my hard-earned bitsies on that?

Yes, I'm hostile.

Did you like the story?

I disagree. I think it did reveal the real me. The 'real me' tells stories. That's the deep and wide of it. Understand this: I don't think there's anything underneath any of us. We're not deep and profound. We're wide and shallow. Pools and puddles like you get after they make it rain here. Pools and puddles and little streams running between them. We don't know why we do what we do. I couldn't tell you why I made us go on an Adventure. I could tell you I was jealous of Sidibe, I could tell you I felt my home was under threat, I could tell you it was change like a moonquake and I would even admit that, yes, I don't much like change that I haven't officially sanctioned. But those are pools and puddles. There's no deep well from which they all flow. This is the moon. There are no deep sources here. It falls from the sky in drops. There's no one real reason. It just felt right at the time.

You know what makes storytellers laugh? That people really think their story reveals something about the person who tells it. It doesn't. Stories are control. First, last, always. It tells you something about who's hearing it.

And no, I didn't tell you the most scared I ever was.

You can guess. But that's just your guess.

So: Sidibe. In the end there was nothing I could really do to stop the menace from Farside. There never was, without breaking Oruka Ring into pieces. Jair out, Sidibe in. We get on now. We get on pretty well. She'll be getting her wings back in five days' time and she's already talking to them. I'll be back at colloquium and I know I will rule it now with an axe of meteoric iron. We have our own spaces, we've negotiated where they cross and where the boundaries are solid as the roof of the world. And that, I think, is the Rule of Everything: moon and rings alike. Everything is negotiable.

Except, when you think about it, it's not so much a ring as a chain. Links leading off everywhere, connecting everything and everyone. Keeping them tight, keeping them safe. And, you know, you can never break the chain.

Family, right so?

# About the Author

Photograph by Jim C. Hines

**IAN MCDONALD** was born in 1960 in Manchester, England, to an Irish mother and a Scottish father. He moved with his family to Northern Ireland in 1965 where he has remained ever since, through Troubles and peace. His most recent fiction is the Luna trilogy. He has won the Locus Award, the British Science Fiction Association Award, and the John W. Campbell Memorial Award and the Hugo. He now lives just outside Belfast. Find him on twitter at @iannmcdonald.

# TOR·COM

**Science fiction. Fantasy. The universe.**

**And related subjects.**

\*

More than just a publisher's website, *Tor.com* is a venue for **original fiction, comics,** and **discussion** of the entire field of SF and fantasy, in all media and from all sources. Visit our site today — and join the conversation yourself.